The Eleanor

A Novel

Michael Croft

ELJ Editions, Ltd. is committed to publishing works of quality and integrity. In that spirit, we are proud to offer this novelette collection to our readers. This novelette is a work of fiction. Names, characters, places, and incidents either are the product of the author's imagination or are used fictitiously, and any resemblance to actual persons, living or dead, business establishments, events, or locales is entirely coincidental.

ISBN: 978-1-942004-79-0

Library of Congress Control Number: 2024946114

Cover Design by ELJ Editions, Ltd.
Author Photo by Danny Goeschl

ELJ Editions, Ltd.
P.O. Box 815
Washingtonville, NY 10992

www.elj-editions.com

Praise for The Eleanor

With hints of noir and magical realism, and a not small amount of humor, Michael Croft's debut novel set fifty years ago in Reno is a classic study in redemption. The hotel Eleanor is a revolving stage that slowly reveals itself as a place of salvation, a compelling turn for both the characters and the reader.

—William Fox, author of *Reading Sand and Time by Distance*

The Eleanor is a delightful romp through a fanciful depiction of old Reno. Croft fashions a story of transformation and compassion on an unlikely canvas of misfits and quirky characters, rich in flaws and gifts. We experienced a nuance between imperfect human-ness and intentionality. Leland is guided by "Other Power" and like a Phoenix rising from the ashes of his life - The Eleanor - he follows his true nature toward redemption.

—Reverends Matthew and Shelley Fisher, Reno Buddhist Center priests

In *The Eleanor*, Michael Croft provides a novel of stunning poignancy about a man, Leland Powers, with a heart as big as his stubborn streak who feels called to improve his own life by making life better for others. Specifically, he devotes himself to caring for the tenants of the hotel he runs in Reno, Nevada in the early 1970s. Those tenants comprise the "Invisibles," the down-and-outers, the struggling pensioners, the underpaid service staff of the town's casinos, all living on the edge but too proud to think of themselves as being in need. On top of all that Leland tries his best to make peace with his ex-wife, does all he can to support his struggling adult daughter, and finds himself trying to make sense of his feelings for a stranger who stands to change everything.

—David Corbett, author of *Done for a Dime* and *The Devil's Redhead*

Norma

They passed eons living alone in the
mountains and forests; only then did
they unite with the Way and use mountains
and rivers for words, raise the wind and
rain for a tongue, and explain the great void.

Dogen's *Shobogenzo*

Leland Powers was a man with a shovel and a hotel. He was also with Aspasia, a giant bird in the air that he, and only he, could see. Wrapped up inside him was a day's work, one that wouldn't let go. Ever.

In early May he was immersed in the world of rubber bands and counting down the nightly take. The weekend had been a prosperous one at the Eleanor Hotel: a riotous blend of money-huggers from over-the-hill looking to warm themselves with cards and dice sitting alongside those glorious icons of the Reno streets, the ones Leland had always tended to—pensioners, maids, bar boys, and those scurrilous drifters who floated through town on three nickels and a dime. Most days Leland would stand there and listen, taking in the lies and cons and half-invented hilarity, before nodding and slicing the rent accordingly.

Out front he spotted Carly, his ornery daughter with the rebellious ways, pulling up in her rough-and-tumble '72 Seville, the touchstone of her cocktail waitress life. Leland shook his head and mumbled. She was here to talk about his divorce and how the family had finally fallen away.

Two years had passed since Dorothy, his wife of thirty-seven years, had rallied up against him and hightailed it out the door with Harlan O'Brady, a Catholic man who liked pounding nails and expounding on the Word. Leland had hired him to add a master bedroom on the backside of his house, a longtime dream he thought he and Dorothy shared. Shortly after the breakup, Leland's body was overtaken by a strange and mysterious hum. Sometimes it was low and tucked away in his loins. Other times it rode through his chest and belly but rarely into his ears. At its worst its unrelenting grip would spiral through his veins and organs, making him walk slightly tilted to one side.

Once he was on a bench with his eyes closed, thinking his life was about to end. When he opened them, he found a big furry squirrel staring directly into his face. Their eyes locked and Leland thought for sure the oversized rodent was there to usher him into the next life, wherever that might be. He inched forward and closed his eyes, hoping to see long hallways and gates made of gold and most of all knowing he was about to leave the irritating hum behind so it could bother someone else. When nothing happened, he opened his eyes and saw the squirrel widen his and flex his nose before turning and scampering behind a rock. "Fuck-head," he said, kicking a small mound of dirt in the air and muttering to himself that life was growing more and more unfair.

On the sidewalk Carly was a bright light among the many. Radiant and tough all in the same stroke. In the lobby she was white go-go boots and tight leathery pants. Sitting on top of her head was a swirl of red hair wrapped up so high that Leland thought for sure she was about to tip over right there in front of him.

Behind the counter and away from the roar of endless TV, Carly asked. "How did it go, was Mom all right?"

"I walked the plank, what else can I say?"

"I wish you wouldn't talk like that."

"I still wake up in the middle of the night thinking she'll change her mind and come back home."

"Me too, but that's not going to happen. She spent this last week getting ready to remodel Harlan's house."

An hour earlier, Leland had sat in the office of Heyburn, Smith, and Cohen, attorneys of the highest order. With his wife of many years sitting nearby with her hands folded in her lap and her gaze across the room, he knew his marriage was coming to an end.

"Is she still giving piano lessons?"

"Every day, best I can tell."

"And students?"

"They stream through the house, fifteen, sixteen, Monday through Friday."

"And Harlan doesn't mind?"

"Him, complain? I don't think so."

He first stumbled upon Dorothy bouncing high and full of merriment at a frat party not far from the marble buildings and long-winded lectures that dominated the hallowed halls of high learning. Fresh off his family's farm in Idaho, he squished himself into the corner and watched her hands fly across the keys, paying tributes to Gershwin and Porter. It was deep into 41 and bombs had yet to fall on the gentle waters of Pearl Harbor. Students were content to stroll the campus and cheer for their star-struck warriors squeezing out a series of long passes or up the middle runs. What they didn't know was that Leland was burning with a mania for numbers and economics.

Four days later they found themselves sitting side-by-side in the library. She was aflutter of trebles and notes and handfuls of music. He had his nose pressed to the table, nearly sniffing every word of David Hume's *A Treatise of Human Behavior.* Finally he parted his lips and spoke. That led to coffee and a long walk through the hills. She spoke of music lessons at five and how the ivory keys were an extension of who she really was. He walked with his head down and dredged up stories about hay and milking cows before dawn.

Outside on the sidewalk, Carly shook her head. "If I could get away with it, I'd go over there and pop Harlan in the mouth."

Normally he'd try to rein her in. After all, he'd had a lifetime of it. She was one part piss and two parts I think I'm going to crack up just for something to do.

"I think we've got enough to deal with at the moment," Leland said, though he lingered on the thought of blood running down Harlan's face and spilling across his shirt.

"I was so upset the other day, I called in sick. The thought of slinging cocktails and thinking about them was a bit too much."

Carly climbed inside her bulky car and strapped herself in place. Rolling into traffic, she gunned the engine and disappeared around the corner.

§

The next morning the sun bled through the windows and Leland rolled over in bed. The night before had been a rough one. Being free of marriage was not going to be easy, he saw that now. He'd have to carry the burden through each and every day, and worse yet was the hum. By two it had been fully upon him, pouring into his cells and overtaking every thought. He tried squeezing deeper under the covers and willing it away, but the harder he tried, the louder it grew.

He knew the thing to do was to stand up and place one foot in front of the other and make himself a cup of coffee. His one and only thought was of Carly. Long before now, they had entered into an agreement. If she sipped on the end of a bottle, he'd close his eyes and tremble. If she fell, he'd open up and bleed. But he also knew Carly in ways he knew no one else did. The thought of her passing through the horrors of this divorce without taking a drink was nothing more than a silly dream. She would have to take it deep inside and let the Old Crow work its magic until she was on her knees.

After breakfast he drove downtown. He'd have to see her in action, or else the day would be a long one. Surrounding him were the split-level homes he had lived with, the ones with the steady surge of beige and white trim and the bathed-in-the-light porches with the heavy doors and the gold locks firmly on display.

About a mile away were the bars and the old places he had always been with ever since he came barreling out of the potato-drenched lands of southern Idaho. In those days the town was settled and worn. The big splash of neon and the cars running through the valet were yet to come. Instead he saw gambling joints that were dusty and full of smoke. Scraggily men rolled dice and bickered over cards as if it were the natural order of the day. Nothing more than a gawky kid, he would stand outside and dream of plucking silver dollars out of the air like they were shiny drops of rain. Afterward he would wander home and stick his head into David Hume's plea to the world and read until his eyes grew too strained to continue.

The El Matador, Carly's palace of nickels and dimes

with wrappers on the floor, was midway down the block. Inside it was dank and money was on the run. At the end of the bar, Leland spotted his daughter in a gown covered in lace and glitter. Standing next to her was Morse Philips, a rotund bag of bones otherwise known as a boss. On his better days he thought of himself as Romeo to her Juliet. On her best ones, she loathed the very sands beneath his feet.

Even closer he saw a dark smudge lining her eyes and a look that would put a chill into a warm day. No doubt she'd been lumbering in the world of wine coolers while curling up on her couch.

"What brings you out so early in the morning?"

"I needed some air."

"You won't find it here."

Leland laughed.

Carly shook her head. "I'm still trying to wake up. I didn't get much sleep last night. Plus this jerk of a boss won't leave me alone."

Leland heard the rough edge in his daughter's voice. It always came after a hard night of looking for answers that weren't there.

Morse stepped in between them. "I hate to break up the party, but the lady over there by the slots needs a drink."

With that, Carly was gone, the sleek waitress on the rise. Leland found himself in the seldom-sought world of chance, five reels and the hope a few cherries would flash his way. On the fifth pull, the unforgiving masters of luck let loose with a splash of nickels into his tray.

He scooped his money into his hand and turned to see if his daughter had stepped away from her Bardo-like existence long enough to see that he had won a little change. Instead he saw that she wasn't even looking his way. She was standing with her head down, and Morse was taking grand liberties with her ear. At first she turned but he kept jabbering away. There was no telling what he was saying, but what came next was a hellacious brand of rebellion. Carly turned and gave him all the guttural rage she had brewing inside her, which was more than a little. "Why don't you go stick your dick in a meat grinder and leave me the fuck alone."

Her anger played through her like a blast of bad air. A woman by the door gasped as if she was witnessing the last moments of someone's life. A fellow with a mop not far from the end of the bar stopped and stared as if Carly had ripped her clothes off for all to see. Morse gathered up his inner need to be in charge and honed down into a pillar of pride.

"Little girl, you best take your filthy little mouth and vanish from my very eyes."

With that Leland was a feral trickster on the move. He sized up his daughter's dilemma and was ready to drop Morse to his knees. "You can't talk to her like that."

"And she can't treat me like I'm scum."

"Then keep your grubby hands to yourself," Carly said.

"It's time for both of you leave by the back door."

Leland squared off, knowing a jab to the head and three to the belly would take him down like those small-town thugs and bigger-than-average hoods who were foolish enough to wrestle with him when he was growing up. But nothing like that happened. A call to be finished with the silliness slid into him and helped him settle down.

Standing in the shadows was a block of wood, otherwise known as a man in charge of keeping the peace.

Leland knew better than to flick a left hand and follow up with a right cross. He motioned for Carly to follow him out the door and into the alley. There they stood, thoroughly surrounded by broken bottles and graffiti sprayed across the walls of a nearby casino. One splay called to him more than the rest: "Peril and sunshine come and go."

"He asked me if I wanted to come over for a back rub. Can you imagine him and me?"

"So now what?"

Carly burned with down-in-the-glory gusto. She snarled at the thought of Morse wrapping his arms around her and squeezing until she gave in to his down-in-the-gutter depravity. "He nearly stuck his tongue in my ear." Before Leland could speak, she went on. She cursed the very ground the El Matador stood on, along with every club through the long haul of what Reno had to say. Her words came so fast and furious that her eyes welled and her mascara ran down her cheeks in long drippy runs. At that very moment, she let go with all the muck and mire that had always plagued her. With it came merriment and release, pandemonium and soul. Left standing was her one and only true self, fragile and yearning, one riding into the other with no resolve, and what came next was clean and clear. "I'd rather be kicked in the head by a moose than go home with that piece of fudge."

§

That evening Leland took to his home and all the ways it was anything but a cozy one. Sitting on a wooden chair, he steadied his gaze on the filmy dust on the red fireplace that was meant to warm him and Dorothy through those cold winter months. He figured if he stared long enough, any reminders of Carly and the ugliness of the El Matador might up and run away.

After a long time, the phone rang and Leland picked it up, knowing Carly would be on the other end, sick and lonely and most likely drunk. She'd want to rehash her day with Morse Philips and why she'd had to tear into him. Instead he heard the booming voice of his older brother, Thaddeus. He was a man who had found his home right there on his doorstep and his path down the road in the form of an LDS Church.

"How are you getting along these days?"

"Slugging it out day by day."

"Has the divorce been finalized yet?"

"We signed off on it the other day. Dorothy and I are no more."

"None of us really knows what the next day has to offer, do we?"

"Have to say, I never saw this coming."

"You have to learn how to steady yourself."

And steady was something his brother knew well. Burning weather, half-grown crops, and dying cows, he rode through it with beatific calm.

"What about Carly? How is she holding up?"

"Carly is being Carly. She likes flirting with the edge."

"Some of us find our way in suffering, there's no other way around it. It's our job to keep a close eye on them."

"I'll have to be careful she doesn't poke it out."

"And the hotel, how's that coming along?"

"We keep plugging away. Somehow we've managed to keep the place pasted together."

"Maybe it's time for a change of scenery."

"Meaning?"

"Why don't you come up and give the farm a good hard look? With some luck, maybe it can clear some of the muck out of your mind."

"I can't do that, not right now."

"Home is the only place where you can find yourself again."

Leland didn't venture into what Carly had put he and Dorothy through with late-night shenanigans and a string of over-the-top phone calls. "Maybe the countryside can do me some good."

"When can we expect you?"

"How about the first of the week?"

"I'll be looking for you."

§

By morning he was hurling his way up the road, but the hum was riding in his chest and flirting with his mind. His only solution was to let it live inside him and stop trying to run away from what it was doing to him. Yet mile after mile nothing helped. The pinging was there to stay.

Through the swings in the road, he finally came upon the darkening lands and the low sling of mountains that held nearly all the farms in place. Soon the old homestead came into view. Small and quaint and nothing more than a kitchen with three rooms off to the side, none of them larger than the ones he rented at the Eleanor.

But it was the old bunkhouse that caught his eye. Home to seven beds that he and Thaddeus and his other brothers had shared, it was there that he would lay up at night and gaze into the stars and linger in a dream world of his own making.

Standing in the driveway was Thaddeus, friendly and wide and wearing a pair of overalls that were faded and ready to be given away. Neither man offered up a hug. Doing so would have been a betrayal of the stoicism that had seeped into them early on.

"You made it, I see," Thaddeus said.

"The pick-up did most of the work."

The two men dithered on about the ride and how the old place across the way was sold to someone of differing faith. None of their words rose to more than a drone. This was how they'd run through most of their days and some of their nights when they were nothing more than boys fooling around the farm.

"Look over there. It's everything we hoped it would be."

Less than three hundred yards away was a sprawling temple built with the help of fellow worshippers and the sweat and toil that fell from Thaddeus's brow.

"Come with me, let's take a walk into the fields. Gladys and her friends are inside talking about one of the boys who's thinking about going sideways."

Up the path and away from the home, Leland and Thaddeus came upon a spread of land that had carried the family along all these years. Corn and hay filled the fields from the base of the mountains all the way down to where they were standing, and on the far side were rows and rows of potatoes, the only crop that filled Thaddeus's pocket with some hard-earned cash. And not far away were a hundred head of cattle, housed and ready for slaughter when their weight seemed true and right to his touch.

"I have to say it feels good to be away from the crazies," Leland said.

"I can't imagine starting over."

"It's the house that's eating me up. I roam until I can barely stand it anymore."

"Maybe you don't have to."

"What does that mean?"

"Gladys and I have been talking. We sure could use

some help with the place."

"Me, a farmhand. I don't see that happening."

"Not a farmhand, a partner. If you come home with some cash, we could buy more land. As long as we can grow potatoes, we'll be all right."

"But sell the hotel after all these years. I don't see how I could do that."

"As much as we want some things at times, they're simply out of our reach."

"But I've got Carly to think about. I don't see her tooling around Burley in a Cadillac."

"Maybe it's time she got out of those casinos. They can't be good for anyone. Some church life might do her some good."

"She's got an ornery streak in her. No telling what might come flying out of her mouth."

"I'm pretty sure I've heard it all by now."

Leland thought of the day at the El Matador and how Carly's fit in the alley made him fear she might come unglued one of these days.

"How about if we let the offer stand."

Leland turned and gazed across a field growing in the afternoon sun. Maybe Reno had done itself in and it was time to stop running Harlan and Dorothy up the flagpole with his mean-spirited rants.

"Best we get some food in you. Always helps to have a full stomach when you have a lot on your mind."

Inside he was surrounded by nephews and nieces, a sea of small faces staring up at him with glee in their eyes. It would take the better part of the day to figure out who was who and if he could remember their names. And on top of that, visiting all his brothers and sisters, who were flung up the road and out into the valleys, would stretch into a day or two of sitting down and getting caught up.

Standing in the kitchen and stirring a pot of gravy was Gladys, Thaddeus's wife of nearly thirty years. "You know Leland, we think of you all the time."

§

The following morning, the whole of them set forth, Thaddeus and his world of Mormon blood, eight all told, trailing after him. Leland swung along through the middle, telling himself it was time for a new experience.

Across the way the temple rode high and mighty, the center of everyone's morning. Bigger-than-life station wagons rolled up on the place and out stepped a bevy of beards and women in solemn-looking dresses. Friendliness was there, but it wasn't wildly on display either.

Inside, the temple was large and filled with wood. Pews were shaped and fastened to accommodate the masses, and there wasn't a single cushion to be found.

Thaddeus directed them to the front pew, where they filed in seat by seat, with him taking the one closest to the aisle. Several members greeted him with smiles and a few pats on the back. None of them recognized Leland, nor were they introduced. The legend of the contrary boy who had fled the fields for the open range of dollar-to-dollar living had long faded by now.

Once the room settled down, Thaddeus took to the podium. His manner was calm and still. Behind him sat a small choir, three women and a young man. Thaddeus welcomed his fellow travelers with a smile and a few words of generosity. "It's nice to see you all this morning. We'd like to open with a hymn. Number 216, 'We Are Sowing.'"

Smooth and perfectly harmonized, their voices filled the hall. Leland closed his eyes and listened, but he couldn't help but conjure up thoughts of Dorothy's piano playing right along with them.

Finished, Thaddeus and the others rolled into the invocation. It was Jesus this and Jesus Christ that. There was no whooping or hollering. No one let loose with any tears. It was all delivered in plain language. Thaddeus said that Jesus would be with them if they trudged a mountain pass covered in snow. And he would also hold their hand if they should ever enter the Kingdom of Love.

Leland sat there and couldn't help but fight in his own silent way. Everything was a bastion of do it upright or do it down wrong. With that he couldn't help but think of the hotel, a place where no one ever did it upright, or so it seemed. It was nothing more than hangovers and dirty dreams of ringing slot machines and hot plates that barely made it to warm.

He leaned back but didn't like what his brother had to say. Yet fighting every word would have been a grand violation of the way this family lived their lives. He'd already spent too many nights holed up in his house, burning with thoughts of seeing Dorothy and Harlan sitting side-by-side at St. Anne's Catholic Church. Maybe the teachings of Joseph Smith and Brigham Young would do him some good, and maybe his adopted home had dithered in the wind for a bit too long. Potatoes and peas might be the only way to live.

After the pledge to Jesus, there was more groping into what needed to be done around the ward. One young man in a white shirt and a skinny way of talking went on and on about his missionary work in Bolivia, with a bit of daring and bravado to his voice. Another droned on with tales of the sick and lonely who needed some of God's unrelenting help. And another summed up the day with stories of Joseph Smith and his untimely demise in Illinois.

Following him Thaddeus called upon another hymn, "O Thou, Before the World Began." His and Leland's eyes finally met for the first time since they'd entered what was essentially Thaddeus's glorious little temple. And Leland could see the wonderment in his eyes and wanted some of it, but not in this way. He knew he was the toughest of the bunch and that he belonged to his hotel, the Eleanor, which in some sort of way was calling to him through the thick and rumble of what the Mormons had to say.

Outside, Leland took in the blueness of the sky and whiteness of the clouds. His brother rode alongside his shoulder and said, "Did that speak to you in any way?"

"You know me, it takes a while for things to sink in."

§

Back at the hotel he flipped through every page of *The Book of Mormon* and tried being with every word. Some were easier than others. A few were beyond his reach. With luck they would seep into him and subdue the hum that was still wearing a path throughout his body. Once up in Idaho, he nearly broke his pledge to stony silence and revealed his plight to Thaddeus, but he always came up short. He couldn't conceive of his brother understanding that his entire body was under siege. His first night back at home, the hum dipped and roared and he didn't sleep more than an hour at a time.

A page early in the book talked about Nephi, an early Mormon prophet and near-constant warrior who found refuge in the wilderness.

At noon Carly walked in the door carrying a saddlebag over one shoulder. "How was the trip?"

"It gave me a chance to breathe."

"Are you doing all right?"

Leland flashed her the front of the book and shrugged.

"You and the church? You must be hurting."

"Any idea when it stops?"

Leland slipped the book into her hand.

"What am I supposed to do with it?"

"You're supposed to read it."

"Have you?"

"I'm making my way through it."

"And?"

"And what?"

"Is your Mormon blood starting to come alive?"

"Something less than a trickle."

"Maybe we should read it together. You and me, a Mormon underground right here in the hotel."

"That's all we need."

"What about church? Did Thaddeus take you into his temple?"

"I put my head down and listened."

"And?"

"I wanna know why they travel in packs."

§

The clouds opened up and the rains came down. Large swooshes of water filled the alleyway, and Leland feared he was going to be swept away. He set his broom down and opened up the back room. Stacked in the corner were large bags of sand, each one weighing about thirty pounds. Hauling them outside in the storm was more than he cared to think about.

Leland walked back into the lobby and scratched his head. For once it was quiet and the TV was off. The rain had driven the rough ones into their rooms, where they could hide under the covers or sit idly in their old stuffy chairs.

Around four, the elevator door flung open and out sprang one of the lifers from the third floor.

"Leland, you've got all kinds of problems upstairs. The water is about to take my ceiling down."

Leland nodded and knew he had everything he needed, a cause mixed in with some urgency. Up he went, each stride long and sturdy, an icepick dangling at his side.

Sure enough the ceiling was about to give. Long goops of plaster hung down around the light fixture and the bed was covered in large drops of water. Leland hauled the mattress and box springs out into the hallway and went to work. He placed a large garbage can underneath the leak, and climbing up on a chair, he plunged his icepick into the mess and down came the sludge. It poured in long even streams and bled across his face. The smell, along with the thought of defeat, ignited images of Carly and Dorothy and how the family had crumbled before his very eyes.

After the water drained, Leland ventured into the elevator and rode to the roof. By now the stars were out and the clouds were moving in an easterly fashion. Not far away was the flash of the casinos. Tall stacks of neon glowed through the night and cast a faint glow across the top of the hotel.

The rain was still a drizzle and the thought of getting sopping wet never crossed his mind. He stood and stared at the long stripes of tar across the rooftop, nothing more than scars from other nights and other storms.

A minute or two passed and he found the crease he was looking for. A slight gash had opened up and let the water flash inside. He scrounged up a sheet of plastic and held it in place with a long row of red bricks.

Sitting on the ledge, he stared down at the street. Cars were whizzing by and the sewers were nearing the top of their capacity. He closed his eyes and listened to the growl rumbling through him now more than ever. He let the roar of the engines come inside and mix with the mess he'd been living with ever since he'd been bundled up and set aside. His mind lathered up and reaped with a dullness and a glory he had never known until this flea-bit moment of hearing the hum sparkle and decide to flush its way up and into the air in crystallized form. What he saw was Aspasia, a giant bird woven out of memory and cast in a brilliant splash of yellow, red, and gold. She bore into him, bedazzling and ready to go. Locking in, she held herself in place for one, two, but hardly more than a beat of three. Then she was gone, back into the light but was never far away.

Leland sat there, mesmerized and alone, but he heard her name, Aspasia, rippling through his mind. She told him the tiny particles in his mind had been sliced through and rearranged. Most likely he'd never be the same again. He stood up and rode the elevator back to the lobby and into the safety of his hotel, forty-nine rooms of broken dreams with a bath down the hall.

§

By summer he put his mind up where it was free and let the quietness come down upon him. In the mornings he would wander his way to the grey depository, otherwise known as a bank, and hand his money over to them. Along the way he would stop and stare at the wide expanse of the river or give a young girl pushing a stroller through heavy traffic a second glance. At the bank the teller would always offer up a friendly smile as she fluttered through the nightly take with Leland knowing that every bill had passed through a lot of hands before coming to rest at the Eleanor Hotel.

Back at work, it was still money and mayhem. He'd welcome the guests and roll them up the steps and into their rooms, but come winter, when the mountains were thick with snow and the streets were caked with slush, he'd have no choice but to sidle up to the drunks and scrape them free of pennies and write it down as rent. At night he would roll into bed and wonder if Aspasia was ever going to flutter with him again. He couldn't help but yearn for the smoothness of a feather or the dollop of her eye, yet a bird was only a bird. When she flashed above his head, there'd been no talk of prophets or the Promised Land. Nor any dithering about Dorothy and the man she'd gone grooming with, nor any babbling about Carly and boyfriends one, two, three. What she had done was penetrate the dark and brewing life that had been swirling through him, and it came with a flash of his circuitry and a downpouring into the roots of his captivity, before sliding back up into the sky and riding in the looseness and rubble that she and others like her rode in.

On a Sunday Leland sat in his chair and sipped a beer, his one and only of the day. In front of him were the Yankees and Red Sox, guys slapping a ball and running through the grass trying to catch it before it hit the ground. If someone were to ask him the score, he would have nothing to say. His only interest was to thin down the day and have a rest.

Near the end of the game, he heard a car door slam and he glanced over his shoulder. Outside was Carly, his unemployed daughter pulling up in her oversized car.

"I'm surprised to see you home. I didn't think you took days off anymore."

"I don't like them, that's for sure, but I needed this one. I might even take a nap later on."

"I'm not used to seeing you taking it so easy."

"A lot on my mind lately."

"Is everything all right? You're not sick, are you?"

"Just taking a much-needed time-out."

"That's good because I might have some good news."

"We could use some."

"Remember Don Immers, the guy who used to live in the hotel?"

Leland ran down his memory bank, a long ride through the cavalcade of run-of-the-mill discards, not to mention the drunks and thieves who colored the place along the way. Finally he came up with Immers, a long slice of a man who was always up and out the door with barely a word to Leland or anyone else in the lobby.

"He's the food-and-beverage manager over at the ShowCase, maybe they're hiring," she said.

"I can talk to him if you like."

"That might be the golden thread I've been looking for."

"I'll stop by tomorrow after work and see what he has to say."

"Maybe, maybe."

Carly stood up and moved toward the door. "Are you sure you're all right?"

Leland shrugged. "I'm not sure what I'm doing here."

"What does that mean?"

Leland pondered the question like it was one of the big ones we ask ourselves. "I mean this house. What am I doing here? I might as well be living in a tunnel."

"Look, you've been through the wringer. Now is not the time for big decisions."

"It's not so much that, but knocking away in this house is a waste of time. I'm thinking of selling it and moving into the hotel."

Carly's mouth dropped an inch or two. "Say that again."

"The fact is that I feel better when I'm down there and not so great when I'm here."

"But it's a hotel with baths down the hall. You can't live there."

"Says who?"

"Common sense says so."

"Who says we have to listen to common sense?"

"Have you let your marbles roll to the backside of your mind?"

"My marbles are telling me a small room where I can rest is the best thing for me right now."

"But what about the house?"

"This used to be a home. Not so much anymore."

"But you can't sell it."

"Why can't I?"

"Because this is where we lived."

"This place needs money too. I'll have to finish off the back room. And there's always something else. There's less money now. Your mother got the investments, and I'm gonna have to send her a check each month from the hotel."

Carly closed her eyes and grimaced. Thoughts of playing outside and running down the street bubbled up and ran away. The simple fact was the family house was on the downhill slide.

Leland's voice went up an octave or two. "I have to be careful these days."

"But twenty-four hours a day in the hotel. Who could do that?"

"I can."

Carly shrugged. "Me, the voice of reason. Who'd a thunk?"

§

That night Leland took to his room, but sleep was far away. He tossed and turned and through what little light shined in from the streets, he saw what he had, the three or four suits hanging in the closet and a scattering of pennies on the dresser. Since Aspasia had whirled through and lifted off again, his house had gone dry, the air felt musty, and the dishes in the cupboard were hard and awkward to the touch. Even though the hum was no longer with him, and had been transformed into a bird, he needed to slow himself down and let his thoughts come tumbling down out of the sky and wrap him up in one big ball of coziness.

The next day Leland strolled the streets. Tourists and beggars were nearly one. Around the corner and down the way, he saw nothing but lights and action. Cabs were flying by and bellhops were on the bounce. Inside the ShowCase, it was much the same. Drunks and cash were firmly on display. Near the last entryway, he spotted Immers, a hard-working man with a metallic clipboard and a slightly balding head. Surrounding him were three or four waitresses, all eager pups awaiting details about the nightly grind.

Immers looked up with nothing but a mouthful of smiles.

"Leland Powers, what a sight to see."

"Carly called and said you were here."

"Ah, Carly, a real workhorse, is what I've always heard."

"That's why I came to talk to you."

"Is she looking for work?"

"Has been for several weeks now."

Immers ran his fingers through his thinning hair. "This is a big place, we should be able to find something for her."

Leland nodded and shook his hand.

"Is she taking care of herself these days? I've seen her wobble more than once."

"She can work, I'll attest to that."

Back home he slouched in his chair and gave Carly a call. She answered on the first ring. "I think we got it."

"You talked to Don?"

"He said he thought he could work something out."

Carly let go with a scream, enough so Leland wondered if she was ever going to stop. When she finally did, Leland hung up and smiled. Even maverick daughters had the right to laugh now and then.

§

On a day when the wind blew and the clouds billowed across the sky, Leland peeled down the road on his way to his newfound home. In the back of his pick-up was everything he owned, a few boxes, some rumpled-up clothes, and a small bag of knick-knacks. The only things that mattered to him were a few yearbooks and a photo of him and Dorothy on the quad at the university. All the other stuff had been given away, the clothes that no longer fit and the furniture that he was tired of sitting on. Even the dishes went by the wayside, except for a couple of plates and a handful of spoons and forks and maybe a steak knife or two.

Inside the lobby he was greeted by ghostly stares. Not one of the renters bothered to get up off the couch and hold the door for the man who had always taken the rent with one hand and placed the other on the key for the cash drawer. And Leland being Leland, he gave them no mind and solemnly loaded up the old rickety car and rode it to the second floor.

Outside the hallways were different now. The carpet was soft and the room numbers above each door appeared to run along in perfect rhythm. Most of all, he wanted to sink into his day and think his life away.

The one he chose was in the back, away from the hysteria of the guests coming and going like cattle trying to fill their stalls. Opening the door, he found a room no smaller than some people's back porch. But he had what he needed, a bed with a sink hanging on the far wall and a dresser tucked in the corner that was scarred with cigarette burns from a litany of guests who never knew enough to look for an ashtray. Outside was the alley, a stretch of road filled with stragglers and delivery trucks stacked high with booze and several kinds of beer.

§

The next morning he was up by 6:00 and into his robe. At 6:03 he was out the door and into the tub only several feet away. In the shower he pulled the curtain closed and let the water spill over his head and shoulders. The warmth filled his body and asked for more, so he let it happen. The spray was almost endless. He washed under his arms and down his legs. The suds beaded up and swirled at his feet and away they went. The whole time the big toe on his right foot wiggled.

At 8:00 he was standing behind the counter dressed in a dark suit and a somber tie, ready to dig into his newfound day.

"I still can't get used to the idea of you living upstairs."

The inquisitor was his graveyard clerk, Murray, a slender man who liked to work nights and sleep through the day.

"It's taken this long to get my boxes unpacked and everything in place."

Murray vanished up the steps and was gone somewhere on the third floor. Leland turned and buried himself inside his daily habits. Before long, Afra, his one and only maid, came dawdling down the steps. Room 207 was where she lived. The hallways and the other rooms were where she earned her keep. Big-boned and burly, she stared into Leland's face and said, "Good morning."

Leland lifted his head and said hello like only a boss can, two parts friendly and one part held firmly in place.

Afra bored into him like she wanted to slide into his heart and take a look around. "Like I was saying yesterday, I'm more than willing to come in and clean your room. I don't mind."

"Not to worry, it's not a lot of work."

Afra peered into Leland's face, nearly eyeball to eyeball. "Did your wife take your house away from you? Is that why you moved in here?"

"I'm not going to waste my life bumping into walls."

"But you're the owner. Owners are supposed to live on hillsides overlooking lakes."

"Lakes are for swimming in."

"All the more reason you should live by one."

"That's why I took the room closest to the shower."

"Man, that's crazy."

Leland gave her a set of keys, and off she went. From there the day poured on. His bookwork turned out to be one pearl after another. His numbers fell into place without fuss and worry, and his pencil felt fine in his hand. To his delight he discovered his flophouse dream of living the way he wanted to was going to finish ahead of the money. Not by much but by a drop or two. Going into the months ahead, nip and tuck was still the order of the day.

The more the sky turned white, the more Leland clung to the couch in front of the lobby and decided to wait out the everlasting blast of snowflakes coming his way. Soon he had no choice but to pace until he could pace no more. He found himself yearning for a country store. One where he could flip the sign closed and call it a day. But hotels were meant to burn on no matter what the weather held. The big bright sign in the front window, The Eleanor, beamed through all the nights and into the days like a beacon out at sea.

Walking behind the counter, he took a look around. And for the first time, he didn't care for what he saw. The back desk was one pile of junk after another. Registration cards, some as old as eight years, were stacked up high in the corner. The rest was newspapers and old ledgers. The drawers were nothing but wrenches, knives, and screwdrivers crammed tightly in every one of them. Underneath, where people typically put their feet, a large bag was overflowing with rubber washers, some so worn and dirty looking that there was no way they'd ever hold water in place.

He had no choice but to put his head down and go to work. Grabbing a bunch of water-stained boxes, he ran them to the basement and stuffed them into the corner. Rattling through the tools, he kept some and tossed others in the trash. Back downstairs he rummaged through several suitcases back by the furnace. Finally he found the one he was looking for, an old tattered mess filled with discarded bars of soap. Years ago he had instructed Afra to save every one of them. No way was he going to run to the store and plop down $1.75 for a box of Spic and Span if he didn't have to.

Upstairs he tossed a handful of bars into a bucket of water and stirred until a crest of soap floated to the top. He wiped and wiped until he could wipe no more. Then his own rhythmic nature took over and off he went. Up one side of the desk and down the other, he was in a bright glow of his own making, and he worked until it glistened and the smell of soap hung in the air.

Outside the storm blew on and the snow piled up against the building. Tomorrow would bring a giant broom and a long wool cap and the muscles that went along with it.

§

A few days later the sun crept out and what Leland liked was that tourists flowed into the lobby one after another. Every one of them had a suitcase in hand and the cash to go along with it. He greeted them with a smile on his face and a handshake when it helped. At noon he took a tally. Five rooms were added to the guest list. With luck he could add five more before the end of the day and call it one big day of fun.

Shortly after one, Dorothy walked in the door and Leland's heart took a long ride to the bottom floor.

"I was downtown, so I thought I'd stop by."

Her steps were soft and smooth, and the smile on her face was a small crest of friendliness, though Leland had to look hard to see it.

"Nice to see you, Dorothy."

That's the best he could do.

"I've been talking to Carly and she said the house finally sold."

"We closed the other day. I'm not sure how many people looked at it. Most of them didn't care for the back bedroom. I guess it was pretty much a forced way of living."

"You did finish it off, right?"

"I found a guy in the newspaper. Turns out he knew what he was doing."

"We're both sorry so much fell into your lap. I never wanted it to be that way."

"It's like the Big Change was upon us."

"I understand you're living upstairs."

"That I am."

Dorothy stared at him quizzically, "And you're comfortable living here?"

"I like it. It's cozy. Besides, it gives me a chance to work on the place. Look what I did the other day."

Leland motioned her to walk behind the counter and take a look at the desk. "Huh?"

Dorothy's eyes blew wide open. "Amazing. What did you do with everything?"

"I put every piece under the ray of light and decided if I needed it."

"Are you all right? This isn't like you."

"I don't know what got into me. But cleaning up the desk got me going."

"Have to admit, it looks like it's brand-new."

Leland cleared his throat. "Have you talked to Carly lately? I was hoping she'd stop by today."

"She calls nearly every day. And it's always the same. Don did this and Don did that. I've never seen her so bubbly."

"I get the same treatment. It's hard to get a word in sideways. You'd think the guy was royalty."

"Least she's not drinking."

"Best I can tell, she hasn't had a drink since she met

him."

"We'd know if she had, that's for sure."

§

That evening Leland sat in his chair and read the paper. The big story on the front page was the opening of a new casino, the Silver Jewel, on the north end of town. Leland tried zeroing in on the fact that there were now more rooms for people to hole up in, but his mind wasn't up for the challenge. Seeing Dorothy had run his motor dry, and he didn't want to think too deeply about his recent debacle with his former wife.

At seven there was a rap on the door and Leland quickly rose, though his mind was firmly on a good night's sleep. Opening the door, he saw his daughter and her more than eager boyfriend standing by her side.

"What do you know," he said, mustering the charm and gusto of a man standing in the entryway of the Taj Mahal.

Carly and Don stepped into a room, ten by twelve, filled with neatness and solitude. The window was open, and a soft breeze rippled through the blinds. With it came the chatter of several people wandering down the alley.

"Sit, sit, make yourselves at home."

The only option was the bed. Don and Carly plopped at the far end and stared directly at Leland, who was settling into his chair like it had been made to order.

"What brings you out at this hour?"

"We're on our way to a movie, so we thought we'd stop by and see how you're doing."

"Sleepy, other than that I'm fine."

"You look good, more rested than you have."

"I saw your mother today. She stopped by for a visit."

"How'd that go?"

"Not bad, we only talked for a few minutes. I showed her where I cleaned up the back desk."

"I thought it looked different."

"I'm not sure what got into me."

Carly leaned into her father with a good, hard look. "Do you like living here?"

"So far, so good."

"We could look for a smaller home. Something close by."

"The last thing I need is a room full of space."

"But you don't even have a bathroom to call your own."

"The heck I don't. It's right outside the door."

Carly closed her eyes and let the steam roll through her. "If this is what you want, then this is what you want."

"Clutter, I swear it's going to be the downfall of the world."

Don stood up like he needed to clear his head, "Maybe we should go. I don't want to miss the first of the movie."

"No need to run off. I want to hear about the ShowCase. How are they treating you these days?"

"Now that Carly's there, my life is pretty easy. When need be, she can cover two sections, when most girls are lucky if they can do one."

Carly preened, "I get going and I can't stop."

Leland beamed, taking pride in knowing that in some ways he'd raised his daughter the right way.

"Don oversees everything on swing shift, and what I like is he respects everyone who works for him."

"That's something this town never gave much thought to," Leland said.

"It's about the money and nothing else. Upper management tells me to hold down labor costs. The casino manager, the guy I answer to every day, tells me to hire more waitresses. They want everyone drunk and happy."

"I'm glad I don't have to contend with anything like that. Here I'm captain of my own ship."

Don glanced at his watch. "We should get going."

He opened the door and stepped into the hallway. Carly was only a few steps behind. Leland stood in the doorway and watched until they disappeared somewhere near the elevator.

§

Leland slept long and well into the night. His pajamas were loose and free to his liking. By two he had squirmed to the very middle of the bed and fallen even more deeply into a cave of his own making. His breath was smooth and even to the touch. At four-thirty he rolled onto his left side and flirted with some dreams of great fortune, but he couldn't quite bring them up into his full being. A little while later, a garbage truck came rolling into the alley and stopped right outside Leland's room. Within seconds he heard the loud hissing of brakes, and the clanging of cans, and a guy yelling out, "Hey, don't forget the one by the door."

With that Leland blew wide open. He blinked and threw back the covers. Accepting defeat, he crawled out of bed and into a pair of jeans and a blue work shirt. The brown suit and narrow tie would have to wait until later in the day.

Fully dressed, including a pair of shabby old hiking boots, he sat on the bed and stared at the clock. It was only a little after five. He had three hours until he was supposed to be downstairs and ready to work behind the counter. He thought about walking up the street and getting a cup of coffee and some scrambled eggs, but it was dark outside, and besides he wasn't that hungry.

Lying back down, he closed his eyes but sleep was nowhere to be found. What he did find was the low-riding musty odor playing games with his nose. He'd spent the last two days trying to figure it out, but it was beyond his ability to think in that way. He had no choice but to clamp his nose down and breathe through his mouth. A second of that, and the riddle was solved. The smell was in his hotel from top to bottom. It was in the carpets and in the walls and most of all in the air that everyone breathed. And everyone, from derelicts to maids to tourists off the street, but most of all to Leland himself, was responsible for fouling the air inside the Eleanor Hotel.

He stepped into the hallway, there among the creaks and the cracks and the smells that were driving him up and out of bed at such an unseemly time of day. He opened the door to the maid's closet and there it was, bold and upright, a Hoover vacuum, the answer to the problem that plagued the noses of every man or woman who walked through the doors of the hotel drunk or sober.

He rankled it out, old and crappy as it was, and plugged the cord into the room and hit the switch. On cue it hummed like a pack of birds in the nearby trees. He pushed and prodded, first around his room and then down the hallway. Each stroke was firm and to the point, and he covered the same patch of carpet over and over, making sure he was digging deep into every inch of the tired old fabric.

Near the staircase leading up to the third floor, images of shampoo with lots of suds swam through the back of his mind. Until now he had never thought of looking into the world of soap in any meaningful way. Carpets and walls and people in the street were not meant to glisten but only to endure.

Slowly lights in the various rooms rippled on, one after another, like they were tied to a giant string. One long-time guest, Mrs. Dauer, an older woman in a shabby gown and a face rippled hard with wrinkles, opened her door and stared at Leland in silent contempt. He stared right back but was careful not to glare. Their eyes were firm and decisive, one beaded into the other in near-perfect harmony. Then Leland was the first to give in. He clicked the vacuum off, and the high hissing sound disappeared, and Mrs. Dauer did much the same, closing her door and shutting off the lights in her room.

Leland stood in the hallway, lost and forlorn. Without question he had quarantined only a little bit of the dust he'd come hunting for. Quietly the hotel returned to its original state of somber. Nearly all the lights in the rooms blinked off and Leland heard the soft wheezing sound of a man snoring in room 222.

Yet Leland was Leland, a driven farm boy somewhat in disguise. Options played through his mind. Vacuum later in the day. Ask Afra to dig a little deeper and aspire to be more. He could even do it this evening before his bevy of guests laid their heads down to his cheaply bought pillowcases and stiff, wrinkly sheets. Then he slipped into the darkness of his own desires and turned the vacuum back on.

In thirty minutes or so, he was finished with the second floor and was onto the third. He heard a few doors open and close, but what could they do? He was the owner and they were the knaves who paid by the week and sometimes by the day. Like it or not, he was a lonesome king in his own pasture.

He hauled the vacuum back down to the second floor

and locked it up where it belonged. Turning, he was confronted by an ornery Murray, standing there full of breath, barely able to hide his disdain.

"You've got the place in an uproar. The switchboard looks like it's on fire."

"I had an itch, so I scratched it."

"But the sun isn't even up yet."

After a brisk shower and a long shave, Leland was back downstairs and into the daily task of money and chores. When no one was looking, he took a damp cloth and ran it over the couch and chairs at the far end of the hotel. Soon Afra was standing at the counter. Leland wondered if he should tell her he'd had his way with her Hoover or if it were best left unsaid.

He remained mum, handing her her keys and mumbling good morning. Idle chit-chat would only confirm he was a cheater of the lowest rank. Not long after she was in the lobby again. A deep husk had settled into her voice and her eyes looked hard and irritated.

"You've got a lot of angry people upstairs. They said you vacuumed both floors at five in the morning. I must have been so far off into dreamland I didn't hear a thing."

Leland groped for words but none came. He stared at Afra, then over at the door. "I thought I was doing you a favor. Save you from having more work on your hands."

Afra's body sagged. "It's more like you're saying I'm not doing my job."

"I'm not saying that, but it might be time to muscle up around here. There's a musty odor I'd like to get rid of."

"That smell has been up there for as long as I have. How come you never wanted to do anything about it until now?"

Leland counted to five and accepted that he had it

coming. "It's living here, that's the difference. I smell it in my sleep. I smell it when I get up in the morning. I'd like to get rid of it."

"I've smelled it every minute of my life."

§

After the blowout with the Hoover, Leland took to the park and skipped rocks across a narrow stretch in the river. Nearby a gaggle of geese nibbled at bugs tucked away in the grass, while two of them stood guard but barely paid him any attention. He tossed one rock after another. The best was a smooth gray stone that flew out of his hand and took flight, skimming across the surface before slipping away and settling to the bottom of the river.

Work had been what it was, but his crew of regulars held him at bay. Reliving ballgames strike by strike went by the wayside. So did talk about who had won at Keno or scored big with one of the slots. What was still there was the smell. Without a doubt, it had saturated his clothes and kept him pinned down. One night he had a dream that a giant glob had invaded his throat and nearly choked him to death.

Staring at his last rock, he gave it a hearty go but before it grazed the water, he spotted Carly's Cadillac pulling up to the curb less than fifty feet away. The thought of company didn't sit well, even with his own daughter. He wasn't in the mood for hearing about romance and pink clouds. He wanted to be alone and ruminate with the dust.

He watched her come charging across the morning grass with him purely in her sights.

"I thought that was you sitting there."

"I came to get some air."

"Aren't you cold? It's still a little nippy."

Leland was done up in faded dungarees and a blue

shirt.

"I'm headed over to Don's, we're going to drive up to the lake for lunch."

"Tahoe can be a lot of fun."

"He needs to get away. Seventeen days straight until now. They must be priming him for something big."

"Is that what he wants?"

"He's good at what he does, that's for sure."

Leland stood up. "I guess I better go home and get ready for work."

"How's it been over there lately?"

"Renting four or five rooms a day. That's enough to keep me busy."

"You know Afra came walking through the ShowCase the other night. She was pretty upset. Something about you implying she wasn't doing her job."

"I never said that. I vacuumed the hallway for her, that was it."

"She said a lot of people were mad."

Leland mumbled a few words before he righted the ship. "Okay, I made a mistake. I went too early. Some people got rustled out of bed. They won't die because of it."

"She said something about putting some muscle on the place."

Leland turned and marveled at three ducks lifting off the water and into the sky. "I just wanted the dust to go away."

"You know Afra is like family. We can't throw her away like she's an old dishrag."

"It's my dust, isn't it?"

§

Another day, another something. At 7:55 Leland held

forth in his own lobby and listened to Murray babble on about a broken-down old man who had gotten confused and sought refuge in the basement. He rooted through some boxes before making a bed out of them and collapsing into a big drunken mess. It took Murray two cups of coffee and a splash of cold water to get him upright and mobile again.

"What about the dirt brigade? Are they still on the loose?" Murray asked.

"Can't say it's completely quieted down, but it's not like I shot somebody."

"People like things the way they are. They don't need a lot of upset."

Murray disappeared out the door and up the street. Leland took note of the grimace on his face, and he re-created one for himself. Carly and her misguided view was still burning in him, and he wasn't in the mood to file it away and pretend it hadn't happened.

Looking around he saw the lobby was empty, and he took off for the second floor. The smell was there waiting for him and instantly crawled up his nose and hung there like it didn't want to go away. Retreating downstairs, he spent the rest of the day in service to the hotel. With Afra there was only a mumbling of shared words, and with the rest of the irritants, Leland took on the profile of a grump, keeping most of them away and somewhat on guard.

That night he seeped into the smallness of his room and refused to settle into the evening rag and the quietness of the breeze floating through his one and only window. He sat in his chair and did what the old nauseating hum of yesteryear had taught him to do, brood deep and fierce for most of the night.

And doing so he brought the smell to the forefront of

his mind and he refused to diddle with anything else. He pondered until it was rich and ripe, so he moved to his bed and stared at the overhead glow. That lasted for a while, then he shut it off and relied on the lamp in the corner. He thought of calling on Aspasia to slip out of the sky and lend him a hand, but he wasn't a full-blown mystic, more a grunt of a man who fumbled his way through each day. And in that thin moment of emptiness, he rolled over in bed and smiled. He had stumbled on a plan, masterful and long, complete in every way.

§

The following morning Leland was lost somewhere in a trance. He had a giant piece of paper in front of him, and he was working on a plan to corral the old musty odor and shove it out the door. He'd sketched in the room numbers across the top and placed a checkmark next to each one. Right below he ran a long list of figures, and beside them were words like *paint, primer,* and *pans,* along with *sandpaper* and *rubber gloves.* At the bottom was a total he thought he could live with, $2,333. There was no doubt about it; the smell had had its day at the Eleanor Hotel.

That afternoon Murray appeared in the lobby, refreshed and probably looking for some food.

"Take a gander at this," Leland said.

Murray stared at Leland's mirage of figures and arrows, some of them too small to read.

"What is it?"

"It's my plan to run the odor out the door."

"What odor are you talking about? I don't smell a damn thing."

"It's like we're staring right at it, but we don't even see it."

"Whoever heard of seeing a smell?"

"I don't mean see it, see it. But the fact is, it's with us every day and every night."

"Man, this is too much for me."

"Ask Afra. She can talk to you about the smell."

"Trust me, Afra doesn't talk to any of us these days. Not since you chopped her off at the knees."

"I ran a vacuum up and down the hallway."

"Yeah, at five o'clock in the morning."

"So shoot me."

"Don't think some people don't think about it."

"I've got a plan to designate one room, maybe one on each floor as a safety room."

"Say that again?"

"We've got forty-nine rooms and twenty-five are rented on a permanent basis. Those are the ones we're going to aim for."

"I'm listening."

"Tenant by tenant will move into the safety room, and I'll swoop in and give their rooms a once-over."

"What about people's stuff?"

"We'll move it into the safety zone."

"You're going to ask people to pack up and move everything into a room while you play Kelly Moore?"

"And guess what, you're the first one up. I want you to move into 211, and I'll get started sometime this week."

"But you know what my room looks like. I've got boxes and books and clothes I'm planning to hang onto for the rest of my life."

"No one is saying you can't do that. You just have to move everything into 211 for the time being."

"This place is getting to be a bit too much."

§

Leland sat on his bed and stared up at the wall. Stretched across it was an even bigger piece of paper than the one he'd been doodling on the past few days. After his mind spun with joy, he'd run to the local grocery shop and tracked down a long glossy roll to go to work on. When he was all done, he had something to marvel at. There were long columns of numbers and underneath them were times, dates, and detailed moments of celebration.

Down the hallway, at the other end of the hotel, was Murray, staring at a room that was packed to the brim. Leland scooted in and took a look for himself.

"Are you sure we have to do this?"

"We'll pack you off to the safety room, and then I'll shrub it down today and paint and shampoo it tomorrow, and we'll have you back in here in less than forty-eight hours."

"Who is going to man the desk downstairs while you're playing Mr. Clean Jeans? I'm not up for pulling more hours."

"I'm going to do it before and after my shift."

"You're talking about twelve, fifteen hours a day."

"Maybe more if I'm lucky."

§

Leland and Murray gave into the task at hand. First came the bed, then the boxes, big and small and packed away in every corner of the room. After that Leland unpinned the posters of Marilyn Monroe and Humphrey Bogart from the wall next to the sink. Each one was faded and covered with the infamous hotel smell. He rolled each into tiny cylinders and wrapped them tightly with rubber bands he carried in his pocket.

"I better get back downstairs," Murray said.

"Two, maybe three days max in 211, then you'll have a brand-new home."

Leland grabbed his vacuum and went to work. He swept across the floors and dug into the corners. After that he dropped to his knees with a bucket of hot water and some rubber gloves. He scrubbed the baseboards clean and worked his way up the walls. Halfway through his water was brown and smelly. He dumped it out and filled it up again and hit the rest of the room. For the ceiling, he climbed a ladder and cleaned it with wide sweeps of his sponge.

Every now and then, he'd glance at his watch. He needed to be downstairs by 8 a.m., which he did with ease. At 4:00 he was back upstairs and at it again. First he inhaled a sandwich and washed it down with some red juice. Then it was one more time across the ceiling with a mop. Still there was more dirt and grim to get after.

From there it was onto absolute glory, his shampooer, the one he'd picked up at a yard sale not far from his old house and stored in the basement. It was a red-and-white canister that rode close to the ground with a long vacuum-like hose, only larger.

Turning it on, it revved and so did he. He loaded the canister with soap and fell right into work. The foamy suds spread across the carpet in round swirling streams of water. Leland pressed even harder and kept going. He swore the smell was juicing into the air and hightailing it out the door. That night he fell into bed and squished into the comfort of his pillow. Three breaths later he was lost in a world of slumber.

§

He stood in his room with a pencil in hand and a brow filled with wrinkles. Up on his wall was a giant piece of paper with a series of room numbers running across the front of it. Proudly he could say four rooms had been signed off on. There were still forty-five to go.

Downstairs it was more of the same, opening and closing the cash drawer and being smooth with the money. At nine minutes after 9:00, Afra walked into the lobby after a long hour of making beds and dumping the trash. Her eyes were tight, and her mouth was crimped because Leland had asked her earlier in the morning to inform Mrs. Dauer that her room needed to be cleaned, pampered, and enjoyed.

"She says she's not in the mood to be up and out of bed by 6:00 in the morning."

"But I'm on a roll and want to be in there first thing."

Afra's face grew even more worried. "I'm not sure you understand what's going on here. You're upsetting the balance. People don't need to be reminded of who they are."

"And what the hell does that mean?"

"Just because you're having a love affair with soap doesn't mean the rest of us have to be belittled."

"The less this place smells, the better off we all are."

"Why the hell do you think we're living here? Because we're in love with the place?"

"And don't be blaming your problems on paint."

"Don't you think we know who's looking back at us when we look in the mirror?"

She dawdled up the stairs and mumbled over her shoulder, "Mr. Bubbles, Mrs. Dauer is yours to deal with."

He sat on his stool and took a look around the lobby. Of the three regulars on the couch, only one gave Leland a friendly smile. The other two turned with a snarl and pretended they didn't see him.

He shook his head and stared out the window. Living with a smell was the same as giving in to the evil forces surrounding the world. Standing up, he opened a drawer and pulled out a piece of paper. Across the top was the name of the hotel and the words 473 Center Street. Leland chose a pencil, one with a tiny point.

Dear Mrs. Dauer,

It was never my plan to upset
your way of life. I simply want
a better place for all of us to
live in. It's important that our
noses be free from top to bottom.

Your room is up next and I plan
to knock on your door at 6 a.m.
I will be very careful with everything
I touch.

Please understand my agony.

Signed,
Leland Powers

He folded the paper and licked the envelope shut. Upstairs he slipped it underneath her door and walked away. Quarreling with a worn-out recluse whose eyes gave up being bright and alive some time ago was not his idea of fun.

§

That night, Leland sat in his chair and worked through the details of his strange and illustrious plan. The smell was the smell, and that's all there was to it. There was no telling what it had done to his mind and to that of the others around him. For all he knew, it was in every cell of his body and that was the real reason Dorothy left him standing in the road by himself.

Waking up the next morning, he felt the tightness in his belly and the urge to rally up against the foul odor that was rolling around inside him. Dressing in a hurry, he told himself to use what little piece of finesse he actually had, if in fact, he had any at all. Bulldozing his way into Mrs. Dauer's room with a paintbrush in one hand and a bucket of water in the other could be one way of looking at a mistake.

At precisely 6:00 a.m. he was dressed and out the door. The hotel was quiet, if not downright still. The only noise was the faint hiss of an electric razor somewhere on the top floor. To his chagrin, Mrs. Dauer's light wasn't on, and the thought of kowtowing was a form of misery he never wanted to be with.

He knocked on her door and her light came on. That meant she was up and ready for a row. He waited and waited, only to bang away again. This time she opened the door but only an inch. He saw that she was wearing a robe and that she was full of yawns.

"Mrs. Dauer, I'm here to unpack your room. I'd appreciate it if you'd go sit in the lobby for a couple of hours."

She stared at him like he wasn't even there. Her lips were dry and cracked, and not one word flowed from her mouth. For a second, Leland wondered if she were truly alive.

"Please, we need to get going."

"No, I don't want you tampering with my room."

Leland peered over her shoulder and saw what he expected to see. Grimy white walls and a hot plate for warming things up and the occasional sip of tea. Spread across the dresser, like they'd been thrown in a rage, were a bunch of doodads, most of them covered in dust. But most of all, he smelled the smell. For all he knew every odor in the hotel was emanating from some foul seeping machine tucked beneath her bed.

"Mrs. Dauer, this is my room, not yours. All I'm asking you to do is sleep in the other room across the hallway."

"I know my rights and you can't make me move."

"This is the Eleanor, you don't have any rights."

Leland heard a bustle of noise and turned to see people milling in small groups at the end of the hallway. Emerging from the pack was Afra, sleepy-eyed and wearing a robe that was far from new. Right behind her came Murray, charging his way.

"Everyone wants you to leave her alone," Murray said.

"All I want to do is paint."

"But Leland, I could hear the argument from my room. A lot of us are starting to think you're acting like the CIA," Afra said.

"I need to stay engaged. That's how it is for me," he said, not wanting to explain how Aspasia had opened him up in a new way.

"But at the risk of upsetting an old lady?" Murray asked.

Leland turned and spied his otherwise loyal employee.

"Whose side are you on?"

"The side of justice."

"I cleaned up your room. Aren't you better off because of it?"

"I don't know. Who wants to feel like they're awake all the time?"

By now several guests were swarming in the hallway, and Leland envisioned a brawl he couldn't quell.

"Leland, can I speak to you for a second?" Afra asked.

He backed away from the brewing trouble and huddled with Afra near the back steps. Mrs. Dauer was still in her doorway, her body firm.

"She isn't going to be with us forever. I mean, look at her, she's paler than a snowflake."

"And your point is?"

"It won't be too long before we're packing her room up and that will be the end of it."

"I want the smell to go away."

§

Leland rumbled down the road. The day had been a treacherous one and rightly so. He'd had no choice but to slide his soap and a few sponges underneath his bed and stack several buckets of paint away in the backroom. He went about his day with a smile on his face, but for every friendly nod he gave his clientele, he had an equal number of thoughts of hogtying Mrs. Dauer up in her room and remaking her sanctuary of lonely little freedom about five times over.

Luckily Carly called and brought up the idea of dinner, that there was something she wanted to talk about. He said he'd come over, but he wasn't in the mood for any razzle-dazzle that he couldn't solve.

She lived not far away in a neighborhood full of trees and children hanging from their porches. On the corner, surrounded by convertibles and other shiny cars, was the Highlands, a mecca of casino workers and nonstop partying. Somewhere there was always a lot of drinking and an endless string of ramshackle love affairs that never lasted much more than a day or two.

And Carly was always right there with them, whooping and hollering and guiding long shots of whiskey down her hungry way of living. On the nights she was feeling it, she'd spin a joke into the air and let it explode like a giant volley of always needing more. When a party would wind down, she'd settle into the comfort of her front room and rally up the relics of those who had driven her sideways. Leland, her mother, and of course, Harlan played through her in one endless roll. And if she had enough gusto, she'd conjure up the different husbands and weave her way through what had and hadn't happened. Coming into morning, right before the birds were about to sing, she'd tweak her list of folks one last time before letting them rest in the gleaming halls of alcoholic justice.

He knocked on the door and waited. Within seconds Carly invited him into what most people would consider cocktail waitress heaven. Shag carpets, velvet drapes, and a white leathery couch that made her living room look like the set of yet another soap opera.

"Come in, come in, sit down. Dinner is about ready."

Leland walked into the dining area, where it was more of the same. Tiffany glasses and red and white candles that had never once been lit adorned her kitchen table. On the walls were two etchings, one of circus clowns and the other of Hollywood starlets. In all they couldn't have cost more than fifty-seven dollars.

Leland pulled a chair away from the table and smelled the pleasant aroma of his daughter's home-cooked meal. For the first time since moving into the hotel, he wondered about the value of cold sandwiches and over-the-counter casino food.

"I wasn't sure I could coax you out of your hovel."

"I get out every now and then, if need be."

"I hope you brought your appetite with you."

"I most certainly did."

"Voilà," Carly said, setting a platter of roast beef, steaming and full of juice, in front of her father. Next to it she placed a bowl of mashed potatoes and a side dish of gravy. On the second trip, she carried a plate brimming with black-eyed peas.

Leland savored the food and asked one simple question. "What's up, what's the big occasion?"

Carly nearly blushed, which was something that rarely happened. "Look what Don gave me, an engagement ring. I would have thought by now that the two of us were married out."

Leland stared at the finely crafted jewel and marveled at how it glistened in the light. "How many times for him?"

"He's logged two but neither one ventured very far into the world of harmony and bliss."

"That makes five that have gone up in smoke."

"Remember, you're in the smoke too."

"That I am, but I'm assuming you've said yes?"

"Why wouldn't I?"

Leland wondered if it was time to let go of directing his daughter's every move. After all, he'd had a lot of practice. First up was George, the part-time carpenter who liked building things and rolling dice. Then came Lance, a man who sold fire equipment and listed five different savings accounts in five different states. One day Carly let loose with a wisecrack aimed right at the psyche of her husband's best customer about him wanting to install an alarm in one of his nine lavish bathrooms. The man was deeply offended and ran out the door, leaving Lance to scamper after him like they were lovers lost inside a misunderstanding. The last one to venture down the aisle was Riley, a coach who lingered for only six weeks, before catching a self-righteous look at one of Carly's intergalactic tantrums and hightailing it to a monastery on the outskirts of Denver.

Nearing the end of dinner, Carly thought of something different to say. "I haven't seen Afra come through the club in a while."

"The sage is busy dispensing her wisdom."

"Meaning?"

"I tried painting Mrs. Dauer's room the other day and it blew up in my face. If it weren't for Afra, we'd probably be at war."

"What's Dauer have against paint?"

"She's a mud dweller, like the rest of them."

§

Early one morning Leland was polishing the furniture and staring at the smudges on the front window. He heard the elevator open and turned to see Mrs. Dauer stepping out of the car, encased in a long black coat and carrying a thinly shaped cane.

Neither she nor Leland spoke. He dropped to his knees and wiped the radiator near the front door clean. Dauer passed by, each step measured and barely more than a couple of inches. She glanced down at him and spoke loud enough to be heard but short of a command.

"We're still wondering if you've come to your senses, or if you want to wash us all away."

Leland didn't say anything. The standoff in the hallway had left him feeling ugly and lost somewhere inside the world of dust. He told himself he was nothing more than a member of the tribe, no longer in charge of anything or anyone.

Opening the door, she paused as the morning air

spread across the corners of her face. Leland was forced to kneel and gaze into the eyes of his hotel terrorist and despise every pore in her body.

She looked down on him full of scorn, and he had no choice but to clamp his jaws shut and stand straight up and let his washcloth dangle at his side. He drew a solemn breath, hoping it would make him appear luminous and large, and he gave a single command to her. "I hope you have a nice day."

Mrs. Dauer didn't offer a reply. She dawdled out the door and was gone, gobbled up by the flow of traffic and the need to eat a three-dollar meal of sausage and eggs.

Vowing he was not about to be told what to do by some hard-bitten relic of the streets, he beat it up the steps and down the hallway. Looking both ways, he reached into his pocket for his key and opened up Mrs. Dauer's door and discovered nothing had changed. The blinds were pulled and the staleness in the air took on the form of an ugly assault.

He leaned against the doorway and asked himself once again how he had let an odor sweep through his hotel and nearly overtake it. It didn't take long to come up with an answer. He'd been too busy with the rooms and the people who lived in them, the crazy ones who howled at night and the friendly ones from Sacramento. The former ones smelled and the others did not. And of course, there was Dorothy and Carly to contend with on a nightly basis.

He flicked the light on and stared at the mattress. To his surprise, the bed was made and the pillows were perfectly in place. He grabbed the blankets and tossed them onto the floor. Sizing up the angle of the door, he thought for sure he could carry the bed by himself. Then he heard a knock and turned around. Standing only a few feet away was Afra, a mop in one hand and a set of towels in the other.

"What are you doing?"

"I can't handle living the way we've been living."

"You can't hijack her room without telling her. You know damn well she'll be back in less than an hour."

"If you leave me alone, I can have the safety room set up in no time."

"She's eighty-seven years old."

"But the other room has some sunlight."

"She wears a wool coat in the middle of summer. Does it look like she craves light?"

"I'm not lying down easily."

"You should know better than to try and change her."

Afra wandered away, the mop still in her hand. The bathroom closest to Leland's room needed cleaning. He stood and stared at the mess in Mrs. Dauer's room, then he glanced up and down the hallway and finally said it, loud enough to be heard but only by himself.

"Fuck it."

And with that he dove into his world of self-made problems. He lifted the bed up on one end and hauled it into the safety room only a few feet away. Leaning it up against the wall, he went back for more. Sheets, blankets, and clothes, he hauled every bit of them into the other room. It took some doing, but he assembled her bed and hung her things in the closet and what came next was the brouhaha.

"What the . . ."

Once again it was Afra, her nostrils blaring so wide they looked like they were about to start bleeding.

"I told you it wouldn't take long."

"That's hardly the point."

"Just don't stand there, give me a hand."

"I think we're past the point of no return, take a look."

Leland turned and stared down the hallway. Coming out of the shadows, her cane dragging across the carpet, was Mrs. Dauer. She placed one foot in front of the other and held Leland squarely in her gaze. He stood and felt his drive shudder into coldness somewhere close to death.

Mrs. Dauer stared at the mess inside her room and spoke very softly. "What I ever do to you?"

§

Having finished off Mrs. Dauer's the day before, Leland was up and away by 7:00 a.m. Downstairs Murray was behind the desk, staring at the floor and brushing the tip of one shoe across the other.

"Don't you feel well?" Leland asked.

"I hate telling you this, but I'm going to give you notice both as a tenant and an employee."

Leland's eyes blazed wide open. "What the hell are you talking about?"

"Me and a few others are pulling up stakes. We don't like what you did to Mrs. Dauer. It's a wonder the poor thing didn't have a heart attack."

"You gotta be alive in order to have a heart attack."

"For years everything has been fine here. You're a good man and you've run a decent place and you don't have a plateful of rules to live by."

"And?"

"And you've turned into a fascist."

"Mussolini didn't invent spring cleaning."

Murray mumbled a few words that Leland didn't understand.

"And what's this about a few others pulling up stakes?"

"That's right, we know tyranny when we see it. That's why I called a summit. A good seven or eight of us huddled last night and voiced our concerns."

"Was Dauer one of them?"

"No, we wouldn't roust an old woman at two in the morning. Maybe that's something you ought to think about."

"I didn't run over the top of anyone at two in the morning."

"Oh, make that 6:00 a.m."

"I got on a roll, what can I say?"

"An assault is more like it."

"So, who all is going?"

"My count has seven of us bailing out, not including myself."

Murray ran down the names, three from the top and four from the bottom.

"That's a third of my regulars. I can't absorb that kind of loss."

"That's what you get for snorting Spic and Span."

"Where the hell is everyone going?"

"Right up the street to the Empire, a place where they don't mess with your life."

"It's a dump, it's worse than this place."

"At least they understand the human condition."

"The city nearly closed them down a few years ago."

"I don't know anything about that. Besides, I've already picked out my room. It overlooks the alley, just like you do."

"Does it stink?"

"It smells of human warmth, if you ask me."

Leland felt like he's been gutted by a band of hooligans. "There's no way I'll rent those rooms in the middle of winter."

"I'm sorry, but you've gone off the rails and that's the price you have to pay for it."

Leland stared outside. Snowflakes drifted across his view, and cars were slowing to a halt at the nearest intersection. Murray stepped on the elevator and rode to the third floor. Leland slumped in his chair and let loose with a string of cuss words. The smell had won out.

§

At 3:00 a.m. the hotel was a cove of silence. Instead of sitting behind the desk and listening to the loud grumblings of a tenant coming down the steps or even the scratchy voice of an old bugger yearning for another day's free rent, Leland had no choice but to sit and listen to the thoughts rumbling through his mind. His minions, or many of them, were on the top floors lost somewhere in their slumber, like he wanted to be, back there in his tiny room far away from the suburbs with their perfectly etched lawns and lawnmowers that barely purred.

The day had been long, pinned down as he was behind the desk, watching Murray carrying box after box out the door and into the back of a waiting cab. Up next was the unemployed dishwasher, a solemn man who fumbled through every day stoked on three glasses of wine and little else. Never once did he give Leland a cross word or cause a ruckus of any kind. Once a week, on Monday or Tuesday, his brother would walk into the lobby and pull his check-book out of his pocket like he was operating under a mandate from God. He'd scratch out $22.50 and hand the check to Leland and walk away, rarely speaking a word.

That afternoon five more fled the premises, all of them falling prey to Murray's sermon about Leland's rules and regulations and how he had ripped the soul out of an old woman who had never done anything wrong but smell in her own special way.

After his shift Leland slept a mere five hours before tumbling downstairs and manning up for another sixteen hours of work, empty rooms or ones that were already occupied, it didn't matter. On his third day, he got off at four and walked zombie-like into the elevator. And for some strange reason, he pressed the button for the very top floor, meaning the roof was where he wanted to be. Stepping outside, he let a swath of air blow right through him, and he felt his lungs brighten and his mind clear out some of the fogginess that had been gathering there for days.

The roof was covered in snow, and the weatherman said there was more on the way. The thought of a leak was more than he could bear. First order up was finding someone to take Murray's place and help with the rubble that had spun The Eleanor into madness.

Thirty minutes later, he decided he'd had enough and needed to sleep seven hours or more. He took two steps and saw his daughter step off the elevator. She was wrapped tightly in a leather jacket and had a wooly cap pulled snuggly over her forehead.

"I figured you were up here, I mean I checked everywhere else."

"I needed to see some sky, not to mention a few clouds."

"What's this I hear that Murray is on his way out?"

"Him and several others."

"What are you talking about?"

Leland delivered his tale of woe.

"You're telling me that nearly half your regulars walked out in protest?"

"More like a third."

"But what are you going to do?"

"Have to rent the rooms out."

"With a supreme amount of luck, you might."

"Right now, I need to get some sleep."

Carly lowered her head and walked around in circles. "What is going on here? You're working sixteen hours a day. Most of your rooms are vacant, and you're living in a place about the size of a garbage can."

Leland shrugged and fought back a yawn.

"Do you think you should talk to someone?"

"Like who?"

"A psychiatrist might be a good idea."

"You mean a head doctor? What the hell for?"

"Because it's getting so I can't sleep at night worrying about you."

"What'd I do?"

"You've changed, that's what. Ever since the divorce, you're not the same."

"Trust me, it started long before that. Knowing that every Sunday, Harlan and your mother are sitting side by side at St. Anne's listening to some priest babble on is more than I can take."

"Daddy, I know it's been hard. It's been hard on all of us, but people come through divorces. They move on. They don't become hermit crabs on a mission to rid a tired old hotel of a few smells."

"A few smells, it's a wonder I have any nostrils left."

"But this is just too much to think about."

Leland knew better than to tell her about the hum and how his body had been invaded by a force that had a melodic range of two or three notes. And how that led to this, a cleaner hotel.

"What if Don and I made an appointment with a doctor, would you see one?"

The thought of seeing a shrink made him do that very same thing, shrink. How was he supposed to tell a stranger that a hum had zipped up and out of his body and splayed itself across the evening sky in the form of Aspasia, a giant bird that caused him to root around and take a look at his life like he never had before.

"I saw a bird right over there about a year ago. I wasn't feeling well and then she erupted out of the middle of me and stared me down for a second or two. But let me tell you, she was beautiful, and she's the one that got me thinking."

"About what?"

"Everything, the house, the hotel, even the air we breathe."

"Now you're scaring me."

"Why, because I think my nose needs some freedom?"

"But we breathe what we breathe."

"I want the people in my hotel to feel the tiny little hairs in their noses come alive, it's as simple as that."

§

The air was dry and the sun was up there with the clouds. Leland thought of staying the course and driving into the hills, even dabbing his toes into a shallow stream and letting the coolness overtake his body. Why the hell should he waste an entire day listening to some university-trained doctor babble on about healthy living? Maybe it was time for Carly to saddle up and ride into the world of self-confession and let the doctor take a look at her inner workings and where her wires had been crossed.

Instead he chose the path of family living and turned

into the Dry Creek Medical Center and looked for a place to park. What he saw was a string of adobe-like buildings more suited for the dusty hills of Arizona or the low-slung valleys of New Mexico. Staring him right in the face was a billboard full of names, and every one of them had a splash of letters hanging off the side of them like PhD or more often MD. None of them appeared to know anything about birds and why some flew with colors and others did not.

He searched the list until he found the one he was looking for, Dr. Bill Ransom, MD. Immediately Leland imagined a large column of a man standing in front of a full berth of books, all of them there to substantiate whatever view he might have on his way of thinking.

The office he was looking for was tucked in the back near an old wooden fence and a near-perfect view of the tall, ranging mountains. He walked in the door and what he thought for sure was going to be a rabbit hole of heavily scarred people with bulging eyes and lunatic singalongs about how life had left them hanging on darkened streets late at night babbling to themselves.

What he saw was a bunch of normal-looking people sitting around like they were in any other doctor's office he had ever seen. He gave his name to the receptionist and was told to have a seat and that the doctor would be with him before long. He sat in a stiff upright chair and picked up a copy of *Lifestyle*, a magazine dedicated to pleasure and frolicking on the beaches of Southern California. In the middle was a big spread about young women playing volleyball not far from an endless sea of waves. Somehow the thought of his tiny room crept into him and wouldn't let go. Fun in the sun ran afoul of how he wanted his mind to twitter away when he was lying in bed late at night listening to the creaks in the floor above him. Deep inside his circuitry, he was a man who needed a cause he could call his own.

"Mr. Powers."

Leland looked up from his magazine and saw a tall man with a friendly smile and skin that was white beyond repair. Leland had to assume he was one of those people who only got five feet of sun every day of the week, if that.

To his surprise the man took him into a room that was small and comfortable. There were books on one side and diplomas on the other. The only name he recognized was Stanford, that grandiose palace of wisdom and success.

"Your daughter tells me you've been struggling of late."

"That's her side of things. I think I'm doing fine."

"Have to say she kept me on the phone for quite some time."

"She can talk, that's for sure."

"Apparently you've had a hard time coping with your divorce?"

"It hasn't been easy."

"Divorce is never easy. Some of us take it harder than others."

"Can't say I rose to the top. More like I took a sledgehammer to the head."

"Carly says you sold your home and you're living in a small room in your hotel. Is that correct?"

"I like it there. I like being close to the world I live in."

"You're going to have to explain that to me."

"My hotel is mine. That's where I feel the most alive."

"And why is that? Most people don't live where they work."

"I'm not most people."

"And why is that? You look normal to me."

"I am normal. I just want my hotel to be a better place to live in."

"But why do you have to live there?"

"I can feel the vibe there. That's something my old house never had, especially after Dorothy left me."

"Why do you think you feel it there and not at the home you lived in for so many years?"

"Because it's close and tight, that's how a vibe works."

"Something tells me you're not about to budge."

"I like the sound of that."

The doctor lowered his head and scribbled away in his notebook. Leland flexed his hands and squirmed more tightly into the back of his chair. To his way of thinking, he had scored well in the early rounds and was holding his own as they marched into the fourth and fifth.

"Your daughter tells me you saw a bird. Is that right?'

"Yes, sir. Aspasia, at least that's what I call her."

"How did you come up with the name? Did she speak to you?"

"Oh no, she was more a flash up in the sky. The name came to me right away. She wouldn't stop singing to me."

"Have any idea what that name means?"

"I had to look it up at the library. It means welcome."

"So how did you come to see her?"

"It wasn't easy."

"I'm sure it wasn't."

"It started with a hum, and I mean to tell you that was one of the worst things that ever happened to me."

"Did you hear someone singing in your ears?"

"No, she was in my body, never inside my head."

"She?"

"It felt like she was a she."

Ransom ran his pencil into his notebook one more time.

"How did she come to be in your body?"

"I don't know, she just came. Not long after Dorothy ran off, I felt a hum taking off inside of me."

"And you didn't hear voices?"

"Can't say I have. Was that something I supposed to do?"

"Some people do when they're under a lot of stress."

"Nope, no voices, just a hum."

"And then what?"

"I lived with it for two years. She wouldn't let go. I mean to tell you it was rough. I hope I never go through that again."

"So what do you think happened?"

"Aspasia, that's what happened."

"Tell me more."

"I went into this giant slump that I couldn't shake off. I felt like I had a barbell wrapped around my neck. No matter what I did, it wouldn't let go."

"And?"

"That sullenness turned into a hum. And I don't care what anyone says, that hum was Aspasia."

"Did she tell you that?'

"No, I keep telling you, she didn't speak to me. She flashed across the sky."

"That was it?"

"She zipped up and out of me and took the hum along with her."

"I've never quite encountered a story like this."

"I was on the rooftop of my hotel and the hum was having its way with me and then it happened. I felt this giant surging inside of me and I didn't know what to think.

I thought I was going to die."

"And then?"

"This sensation shot through me, and I saw this giant bird flash up in the air. She was red, yellow, and gold and hung right in front of me for about three or four seconds."

"And?"

"She ran away and left me hanging. I guess that's what some women do."

"And the hum?"

"Gone too. That's why I said she was a she. Aspasia hummed inside of me for nearly two years and then decided to hightail it up and out of me."

"I'm not too sure I know what to say."

"A hum will do that to you."

"Do you think you'll see her again?"

"Hard telling. For all I know she could have invaded someone else's body by now."

"Do you think of her as a real person?"

"That's a tough one. The more I think about it, I think Aspasia was a manifestation of the air."

Dr. Ransom gave Leland a hard look. "Would you be willing to see me in follow-up sessions? Maybe we can dig into Aspasia and see what she means to you."

"Do you think you can convince her to come back to me?"

"I don't think I can make that kind of promise."

"If you don't know anything about the air, then why should I come back?"

§

Leland receded into a bevy of five-dollar bills and woeful tales about why the rent was never going to be paid on time. The first offender was another fallen hero who wanted Leland to listen to every word that fell from his mouth.

"I want you to know I'm going to be a day or two late with my money. I've had this deal brewing with people in China, and it's going to take a little longer than I thought for them to complete their paperwork."

"China, huh, that's interesting."

"Truly marvelous people, it's been a real pleasure working with them."

"And exactly what do they do?"

"They make transistor radios."

"And you help them from right here in the hotel? Now exactly how do you do that?"

"I'm a letter writer from way back, and I have all kinds of ideas about shapes and sizes. I even wrote them a long dissertation on the quality of sound, what it is and what it isn't."

The crafter of this tale was a big man with a sloppy build attired in loose-fitting black slacks and hi-top running shoes. Leland closed his eyes and pondered whether yuan translated easily into American-made dollars. But he didn't dwell there for long. He'd learned long before now that lies were like flies and it was best to swat them away.

"Now, I want you to listen to me," Leland said, leaning across the counter and nearly bumping his nose right up against the writer of the Chinese fiasco. "I want you to go back upstairs and come up with a story that has some truth in it."

The man lowered his head, his breathing turned solemn, nearly pathetic. "But I did send letters to China."

"And I invented the Oldsmobile. Now go back upstairs and see if you can come up with something a bit more reasonable."

An hour later the man was back. This time he stared

down at the floor and mumbled. "I drank up my rent money and I won't have anything coming in until the end of the month."

"Now that's a story I can live with."

The man smiled with a smidgen of delight in how he was acting.

"I need your word that I can get at least a hundred dollars by the end of the month. If not, you'll be sleeping down by the river."

The man nodded and wandered in the direction of the front door. Leland slouched behind the counter and took pride in the way his day had spun in favor of all things bright and friendly. He had tamped down a highly trained but misdirected man of medicine when it came to matters of the light. Anyone smarter than a bag of peas should have known that Aspasia was as real as an antique car sitting on the side of the road or the size and shape of an astronaut's head right before he blasted off into space.

At 1:00 the door opened and in walked Murray. In his left hand he was carrying a small bag of cherries. "I was passing by, so I thought I'd stop in and say hello."

"How's life at the Empire?"

"It ain't like here. Ever since the new owners came in everything is buttoned down and runs on time. No noise, no looking sideways. The rent is due the second it's due, and if you don't have it, you'll be wandering the streets looking for a new place to live."

"Are you begging to get back in here?"

"Me, no way. I pay my way. Besides, they've got me working graveyard just like you did."

"What about the smell? Does that place stink too?"

"Of course it does. Man, that's hotel smell. They all smell like that."

"That's crap."

"What I want to know is why you never bothered with it until you moved in here?"

Leland pondered the question and hardly for the first time. Maybe when Aspasia ripped her way through him, she had sharpened his nose hairs along the way.

"What is the status of the smell? Did you eradicate it?"

"No, it's still here. Let's say it's on hold."

"What about Mrs. Dauer? Did you run her off into the desert?"

"She'll be here long after we're gone, and so will her hot plate."

"I want you to know there's no hard feelings. You're a good man and you run this place in your own way. Least you'll take time to listen to a sob story."

"Well, I've sobbed a time or two in life."

Murray stared at him. Maybe he was calculating the loss of Dorothy and the sale of his home, Leland wasn't sure.

"Here, have a cherry, on me."

Murray held the bag up to the man who had once been his own high-and-mighty lord of the land and let him dig in. And Leland, being cautious about someone who had led a mini-riot right there in his hotel, settled on the largest cherry in the bag. After all, Murray owed him that much. His socially driven assault had cost him more than a few pennies, primarily through the hard-charging days of winter.

He plopped the sweet-smelling thing in his mouth and for some strange reason, the piece of fruit took him on a ride into the far-flung hills of sugar land, meaning he had a rush from one side of his mind to the other.

"Whew! Where'd you get those? I never tasted

anything so good."

"Up at the market, the one next to the Empire. Here, have another one."

Leland reached into the bag and the same thing happened again. His synapsis opened up and asked for more, only this time Murray held the gift close to his chest. Leland had no choice but to go on the hunt for himself.

"Don't wait," Murray said. "They're going fast."

Later, Leland's new clerk walked in the door and sidled up to the counter. His name was Jake and he'd been a hotel man in San Francisco, meaning he knew how to answer a phone and tell people how to pay the rent. Leland showed him what to do and headed for the door.

In less than five minutes, he found what he was looking for, O'Dell's Fine Foods and Even Better Groceries. A small place filled to the brim with apples and beer, not to mention eggs and several types of bread, and of course a morning round of newspapers and right there by the window a full display devoted to nothing but dental floss.

But Leland wasn't there for toothpaste, corn, or skim milk, only cherries, and the bigger, the better. Not far from a large display of bananas, he finally found what he was looking for, cherries the size of quarters. He seized on the biggest ones he could find and marched them to the counter. A Pakistani man, tall and slender, and wearing a bow tie and an ever-present smile, greeted him with a slight bow. Leland pulled a dollar bill out of his pocket and followed up with some loose change, and just like that, the cherries belonged to him.

Outside he looked at the people in the streets and a string of apartment buildings lining the way. He knew only one thing, he wasn't going back to the hotel. The only question was where he was headed.

Across the street and up a ways was the Empire, the place Murray was so in love with. Owned and operated by the Thurman Brothers, a pair of Special Forces who migrated to Reno and opened up a hotel and ran it with military-like precision. For all Leland knew, even the floors squeaked on time.

That depressing thought led him in one direction and one direction only, the park. He needed to breathe in the river and the nearby road and even look at the tennis players who were smacking a ball back and forth across a nylon net. About a block away, he spotted an old woman in a faded dress and her hair up in curlers standing on her porch watering what he thought was a long row of flowers. He couldn't help but stop and stare, and that's when he slid the first of several cherries into his mouth.

Closing his eyes, he sucked until a ripple of juice wallowed inside his mouth and trickled down his throat. What followed was another high of high proportions.

"Can I help you with something?" the lady asked before turning and setting her watering can at her feet.

"No, ma'am, I was out for a walk and stopped to admire what I thought were flowers, but I now see they're tomatoes."

"That's the plan. Now it's up to me and lots of watering."

"We used to grow them when I was a kid."

"That's a good thing."

She stepped off the porch and let Leland stare at her. Her hips were firm and her eyes were pale, enough so Leland nearly got lost in them.

"What do you plan to do with them?" he asked.

"I plan to eat them."

"That's a lot of eating."

"Oh, I'll probably give a few away, but I try to eat one with every meal. That's why I've lived as long as I have."

"And how long is that, if I can ask?"

"I'm ninety-seven today and still doing my own cooking."

Leland was mesmerized. He wouldn't have guessed more than seventy-five.

"Why don't you stop back when things are ready and I'll let you have a few."

By now the sweetness was having its way with how he thought. He couldn't help but let his mind wander and zero in on the plants, each one so wild and free that he knew in the coming weeks firm, round tomatoes would be hanging from all sides ready for her to eat.

§

That evening he was asleep and riding high among the treetops—up there with Aspasia and others more or less like her. Along the way he felt the push and pull of the old irritating hum, the one that yesteryear had so lovingly bestowed upon him. Now it was nothing more than a single blade of grass billowing on the side of the road. Up ahead he saw the old woman's tomato plants and then some. Thousands of them, fertile and alive and baking in the same rich fields of his Mormon youth, the soil that he and his brothers had tilled in the hard and lonely days of spring, trading in their younger years for the toil and tedium of adulthood.

That morning he woke to the bountiful smells of his own mind. The odor of peas, tomatoes, even green beans soothed him with every breath he took. Nowhere was the smarmy lowdown smell that had plagued him for so long.

Dressing, he dawned his regulatory suit and was out

the door. Only this time he didn't take off for the lobby, he went directly to the roof. There he stepped into the palatial playland that had given him so much. Mainly Aspasia and a chance to start anew.

He began walking across the roof in slow, easy strides. Each step was roughly a yard long, and with ease, he envisioned rows and rows of tomatoes, and along with it, the sweat and hard work that came with his homeland when he was growing up on the farm.

§

Downstairs he went to work on a piece of paper. No longer was it pencil marks and wanting to know who had and hadn't washed behind their ears. It was about lumber and soil and knowing how to caress a seed.

He drew a number of tiny boxes and some were bigger than others, but he needed to find the right size if he wanted a rooftop garden.

That evening he was at Mr. Brown's Lumber's dressed and ready to go in a pair of blue jeans and a matching shirt. Both felt smooth and warm against his skin. The days of suits and ties were fading, and he wished he could toss them into the flames of a burning fire. It wouldn't be long before he was rolling in the dirt and turning seeds into brightly lit tomatoes. Anything to free his minions from the hazards of fried foods and over-the-counter hot dogs.

He cornered the first salesman he encountered and went to work on him. "I'm thinking of building a rooftop garden, and I might need your help."

The portly man answered right away. "We aim to please at Mr. Brown's Lumber."

Leland showed him his piece of paper filled with slices and dices. In the middle was a giant box, the centerpiece of his latest craving. In the heart the conversation, he came ever so close to divulging the whole of his plan of having a hotel fortified with daily nutrition counts that would make any dietary doctor stand up and scream with delight.

§

On the first of seven overwrought days, Leland flung the door open to his storeroom and stared at his pile of wood stacked neatly along the far side. Each strip was one by sixteen, all handpicked and free of blemishes. His aim was a box thirty-two by forty-five, large enough for bags and bags of tomatoes, the swelling fruit, the one the gods wanted to be full of health and longevity.

Grabbing only one board at a time, he headed for the roof by way of the back steps, careful not to nick the walls or make any sounds that might find their way into the lobby. He placed each one exactly where he wanted his garden to flourish. After ten trips, he stepped back and stared at his pile of redwood. Nothing more than fallen trees, songbirds, and morning dew would have to wait for a new round of wood coming their way.

With the break of dawn, he began hammering and trying to drown out the cries of screeching cabbies and the gushing sounds of the delivery trucks headed into the center of town. At 7:30, he had no choice but to pull up and ready himself for yet another any of work. Two minutes into the grind, he was confronted by Afra.

"Tell me, was that you I heard bustling up and down the back steps?"

"That might have been me, hard telling what goes on here at times."

"Is the roof leaking again?"

"Not that I know of."

"Then what's all the racket about?"

"Maybe I'm expanding my vision."

"A vision of what, another assault on our warm and friendly smell?"

"Trust me, I'm way beyond doing that again."

§

The second day meant more sawing and the securing of the drain that ran to the back of the roof. Late that evening he anchored his garden with heavy spikes at the corners and in the middle of each side. He even dabbed each with heavy tar, protecting the third floor from leaks.

The next morning was devoted to dirt and little else. Armed with a pair of five-gallon buckets, he crept up the back steps. At each landing, he had to stop and wait for his breath to settle down so he could regroup. Each toss was like a splash of water, covering only the thinnest parts of the roof.

He finished off in the evening by trudging up and down the stairs for another three hours. The following night he carried even more, so much so, he had to rest the next morning. His arms ached and his legs throbbed, and he spent a good hour or more soaking in the hallway tub and was glad no one knocked on the door and asked him to hurry up.

He followed up with his strongest performance by rising at dawn and working until he was surrounded by a bevy of stars. Between trips he used a shovel to smooth the top and firm the edges of his garden. Another ten runs ought to do it, he told himself. Then he could celebrate with a bowl of ice cream with a cherry on top.

Hearing the elevator swing open, he looked up and saw Carly coming his way. She was wearing a long white coat over what looked like her cocktail waitress garb of a satiny costume and fishnet stockings.

"Now what are you doing?"

"A little farming, have to say it feels good."

"But up here?"

"Why not, this is where the sunshine is."

"What do you plan to grow?"

"Tomatoes, and lots of them."

"But how many can you eat?"

"They're not for me, not all of them. You and Don can have some but most are for the people downstairs."

"But why?"

"So they can taste purity for once in their lives. Anything's got to be better than fried food and a dollar-off afternoon meals at the ShowCase."

Carly stared until she couldn't stare any longer. "I just don't get it, why we have to go through this all the time."

"Through what?"

"The selling of the house, you moving into a dump of a room, and your crusade about some mysterious smell. And now this, turning the roof into a farm."

"Tick forward or die, that's what I'm saying."

"I keep hoping one day I'll get my father back."

"I'm right here. I'm not going anywhere."

"Don and I have been talking. Why don't you move in with us? We have plenty of room."

Tiptoeing around a couple of people who appeared to be in love wasn't his idea of fun.

"I can't do that. This is the life for me."

Carly mumbled and turned away. Her walk was hurried, almost spiteful. Leland dug his shovel into the soil and turned over a small mound. If only she knew about the terror of the hum and what drove him through the day, then maybe she'd understand.

§

Leland pulled the covers over his head and scrunched

deeply into his pillow. He wasn't going to carry any more buckets up the back steps this morning. The hard glare in Carly's eye had made for a painful night of sleep. At two he thought of giving up and turning on the light, but he settled his will into place and calmed down. If he sat up all night, he'd be too tired to finish off his box.

Finally he rose at the last possible moment and splashed his face with cold water. That evening, after a bowl of noodles and a glass of milk, he scooped the last of the dirt out of his pickup and ran it upstairs. With a light toss the darkened soil flew out of his bucket and into the air. To Leland's way of thinking, the clouds should have parted and a trumpet blared a long string of freedom.

Instead he climbed into his box and dropped to his knees. The soil was everything he wanted it to be, rich and moist, and tucked inside every particle was the whole of him, his breath, his graying hair, even his brother Thaddeus and the tribe he left behind.

Before he could stand, he heard the door click and he feared Carly was back for more. To his surprise he saw Don Immers, possibly her one and only savior, coming his way.

"What do you think, pretty snazzy, huh?" Leland said.

"Seems like a lot of work for a bunch of tomatoes."

Leland heard the firmness in his voice and saw the single line of action residing in his eyes. "Some things are in the doing. That's what some of us need to understand."

"You can buy tomatoes in any store and that way you don't have to destroy your daughter in the process."

"What the hell does that mean?"

Don held his arms out in front of him and shrugged. "She's off to the races once again."

"So what happened?"

"What happened? You happened."

"Come again."

"The jive, you and a bunch of tomatoes."

"So you're telling me she's drunk?"

"Drunk, she's way beyond that. She's off into voodoo land."

"This started last night?"

"Apparently she had a bottle hidden in the top cupboard. And after that, she went out for more."

"Did you try and stop her?"

"How? She's a bull, just like you."

Leland dusted the dirt and grime off his pants. "Where is she now?"

"Home sick in bed, borderline hallucinating if you ask me."

"Should I come over?"

"I don't know if you'll make it better or worse."

"That's one I've been asking myself for years."

§

Leland rolled through the neighborhoods, finally coming upon the one Carly and her new-found boyfriend had been living their fantasy in. Low slung and wide, their house sat on the corner of a cul-de-sac, most likely home to other casino workers who had ebbed their way into respectability by escaping the comings-and-goings of apartment house living.

Pulling into the driveway, he spotted Immers standing in the living room. Through the shadowy glare, he looked almost ghostly. He was pacing back and forth and carving out a path of no more than a few feet wide. Leland rang the bell and waited for less than three seconds. Immers opened the door and displayed an outcropping of veins flaring through his cheekbones and down into his chin.

"I don't know what to do, it's driving me crazy."

"Let me talk to her."

"Please, no firm demands. That's half the reason we're in the shape we are."

"This is hardly my first glide through these streets."

And with that comment, a flash of alcoholic despair peeled through him like a filmstrip with no end in sight. The first shout-out came early, merely days into her sixteenth year. One evening Leland and Dorothy invited friends from across the street. Champagne flowed and unbeknownst to anyone, Carly sipped a glass for herself. More would have been detected and naturally denied. What followed was fury and lots of it. She let go of all the pain residing in her, and told everyone that they were terrible people and it came with a language of the worst kind, words that seemed to reside in the depths of her troubled soul.

Her next furious spillover was with her first boyfriend, a high school quarterback named Jake Malone. She caught him necking in the parking lot with a little cheerleader named Becky Sue. What came next was a bottle of rum and a run of seclusion that lasted from one weekend to the next. In adulthood there were scattershots of boyfriends and divorces, long nights on the couch, and wine coolers at her feet. In between she could be bright and inviting. Working hard was always her credo, fake furs, and plastic flowers in the doorway her calling card.

Carly was sitting at the breakfast nook dressed in black slacks and a beige blouse. She was staring directly into a plate smeared with soft-boiled eggs and sausage on the side and did not appear to be a sloppy drunk.

"She won't stop talking," Immers said.

"Is that a bad thing?"

"It is when she says the same thing over and over again."

Leland pulled a chair away from the nook and sat next to his daughter.

"Well, if it ain't the farm boy. Did you stop by to give us some hay?"

"Carly, there's no need to talk like that," Immers said.

"No, we have to honor this man. He's unique. He doesn't even have a toilet to piss in. He has to use the one in the hallway."

"Carly, please."

"And it doesn't stop there. He can't simply pull up and be a Mormon like his family wanted him to be. He has to waste his time shoveling dirt on his rooftop."

"It's going to be a good thing. Fresh fruit will help change the tone in the hotel," Leland said.

"I thought you said you were growing tomatoes."

"I am, as many as I can."

"Tomatoes are a vegetable, didn't you learn anything on the farm?"

"Tomatoes are a fruit."

"Watermelon is a fruit. Apples are a fruit."

"And so are tomatoes."

Carly rolled her head in a loopy circle. "One more time, the big man is telling me how to think about things."

"Would both of you please stop talking," Immers said.

Leland mumbled but finally said something worth hearing. "I didn't come to argue."

"Good, because you won't win this one. Tomatoes are a vegetable."

Immers dismissed them both with a flick of his wrist.

"What about work? You must have a shift coming up," Leland said.

"I've been covering for her, but I can't for much longer."

"You need to clean up and think about getting back to work."

"I'm going to quit and grow radishes in the back yard."

"Good for you, I'm going to shower the hotel with tomatoes."

"Do you think your band of derelicts care one iota about anything like that?"

"Decay can't last forever."

§

Late in the week, Leland fled to the dreamy sunlight of his garden. The previous days had been spent nudging and plodding with Carly. If he called her, she refused to listen, always slipping and sliding with comments about farmers and old man descending into foolishness. If he chose to leave the phone alone, she would call him, once, twice, three times a day, her words always a slurry mess and often slamming Immers for spending too much time at the ShowCase.

Closer to the weekend and after another day of filing cards, Leland stood on the edge of his garden shoveling dirt and wanting thoughts of Thaddeus to come rolling back him. Before planting, he knew he needed to find his rhythm, his need to till the soil every morning and then again at night.

Shortly after dark, a refugee from the lobby opened the elevator door and stepped out onto the roof. "Leland, they say you've got a call at the front desk."

"Tell her I'm not here."

"They said you better take this one."

He set his shovel down and rode to the first floor. He swore the eyes of his lobby dwellers were upon him and that calamity fired up their lives.

The line clicked and Carly's voice filled in the void. "Immers kicked me out of his house. He shoved me into my car with all my clothes and told me to never come back."

"You drove?"

"Like a thief in the night."

"You're lucky you're not in jail."

"For what, weaving with perfection?"

"Have you talked to your mother?"

"You mean the carpenter's wife?"

"Something like that."

"She keeps talking about St. Anne's. I think she wants me to marry a priest."

"I doubt that."

Leland ran his fingers through his hair. All he wanted was the touch of soil on his hands. "What about work? You better get down there."

"You mean back to the mothership?"

"You need to earn a buck and find your way."

"Farmer John, I can slither with the best of them."

Leland listened for more. "Carly, are you okay?" A breath was all he needed to hear. "Carly?"

He didn't hear anything and that's all it took for his mind to run with the thought of his thirty-seven-year-old daughter stretching out to the end of her life. He grabbed his keys and was out the door, though he didn't slam his way through the blocks. Instead he chose the easiest way and only once goosed the pedal. At the sight of a light turning red, he pressed down and slid across the lines with the lightest shimmer of a smile on his face.

At the Highlands, he traced her car to the last one on the right. It was straddling several spaces and the door was left open for everyone to see. He shut it with a hard push and knocked on Carly's door. After a few seconds, he hit it again, only this time he called out. "Carly!" Still all he had was the blank slate of the door staring back at him.

Drawing anyone else into the fray didn't enliven him in anyway. He slipped around the side of the building and tapped on her window but got nothing in return. He picked up a rock and slammed it into the glass. A hole big enough for him to reach through appeared and he opened the window.

"You here?" He squinted but finally spotted her, splayed there beneath the covers, her head tilted, her nose upright. "Are you awake?"

He stroked the side of her face, yet her eyes didn't flutter, nor did she offer up as much as a quip. "You need to get some food in you?"

She coughed three times and drew a heavy breath.

"Carly, come on."

What came next was a volley of vomit and a round of choking. Leland tried wiping her face with the sheet, but she gurgled even more. Reaching for the phone, he dialed for an ambulance. He spit out his own brand of urgency and told them how to find her apartment. In less than three minutes he heard the slice of a siren in the early-evening air and walked outside. From down the street, he saw the flashing lights swirling through the air. Two men and a woman, all young, scampered to his side, not one of them flushed with anxiety.

Back inside she was pasty white and at best offered up the slightest of groans. With ease, they rolled her onto a gurney and strapped her into place.

"It's best if you follow us to the hospital," a young woman with short sandy hair said.

At the hospital, he sat in a waiting room near the back of the third floor. Three hours later, a young doctor greeted him by saying, "Mr. Powers, your daughter is a very sick young lady. We're all lucky you called 911."

"Has she come to?"

"She's opened her eyes a few times. We're hoping to have her up and walking by tomorrow."

"Should I go in and see her.?"

"No, we want to keep her calm today."

"Not even for a few minutes?"

"We're still trying to sort through her symptoms. Do you live in a small room with a bath down the hallway?"

"I do."

"And what about tomatoes? Do you grow them on a rooftop close by?"

"That's me again."

"Oh good, we thought maybe she was hallucinating. One of us even thought maybe you were in prison."

§

Though a nip was often in the morning air, a heatwave settled in from the north way ahead of summer. Normally Leland didn't give the weather much thought, but right now he needed a soft breeze to calm his burning mind. If he didn't get some rest, he'd have no choice but to slog his way through the next morning and into the afternoon.

He climbed out of bed and rummaged through his closet, finally pulling his sleeping bag from under a pile of clothes. He hadn't used it since he took Carly fishing when she was only nine or ten. Still clad in his pajamas and with his pillow tucked beneath his arm, he ascended to the roof. Opening the door, he stepped into the hot muggy air and stretched his bedroll alongside his garden.

Drawing deep breaths, he did his very best to take in

the fertile smell of his garden, but his nose was dry and irritated. He knew he was old and getting older. His daughter's flirtations with the great beyond were more than he cared to think about. Even his troubling years with the hum were easier than this. At least his delirium had given him something to do.

He closed his eyes and gave in to sleep but only for a minute or two. Waking, he wondered if his own clock was running out and by morning someone from downstairs would find him sprawled on his rooftop, lying next to his unfinished garden and the thought he'd never planted as much as a single seed.

And that's when Aspasia came for a second time. She lifted out of him and splayed herself across the evening air. Gone were the brilliant flashes of yellow and gold, even the touches of blue were missing. Instead she was draped in somber tones of red and brown and was hampered by a crippled left leg.

He lay there, his breathing slightly more than a ripple, and watched Aspasia hobble in small circles, meditative and alone, and obviously drenched in pain. But before Leland could budge, she was gone, back into the air around her. He'd never know if she would heal in this lifetime.

§

Leland sat on one end of the couch, while Dorothy plopped down on the other side. Fortunately for them, the lobby was quiet, the inmates were still at rest.

"What do you think got her going this time?"

"Tomatoes."

"Excuse me?"

"I've started a rooftop garden, and apparently she doesn't think it's something I should be doing."

"Is this your latest need to stay alive?"

"Soil and soul, you can't have one without the other."

"I can."

"Think of it as my way of playing music."

"So what became of the smell?"

"I gave it a good hard battle, but let's say I didn't win the war."

"I hear you nearly had a donnybrook up and down the hallways."

"I can't help it if some people don't like being helped."

"I better give her a call and think about going up there. Do you have a room number for her?"

"They can give it to you at the nurses' station."

"What about Don, how is he doing?"

"Frayed around the edges and done for."

"Add one more to the tally."

Dorothy left and climbed into her car. An hour later Leland made arrangements to break away from the daily grind and drove to the hospital. Not far from St. Anne's, County General was five stories tall and more gray than white and sprawled for several blocks. Mounting the steps, he smelled the smells only a hospital had to offer, the lotions and the sprays, even the faint odor of people hanging on. He asked a woman in a white cap and a tight-fitting outfit for his daughter's room number. She found her name and directed him to the nearest bank of elevators.

Inside he rode to the fifth floor. Outside he saw the surgeries and a litany of broken legs. Around the corner, he spotted Carly standing near the end of the hallway, her hair in a dither and her knees wobbly and thin.

Leland pressed for something to say but instead kept his gunslinger gaze steadied on his daughter. In the light she looked fractured and torn, the paleness of her skin shining through, at times looking like the frightened little girl he walked down the street to St. Anne's Elementary. Before he could speak, she turned and fled into the safety of her room. He picked up his stride but barely.

"I ate all my Jell-O," Carly said.

"You did?"

"Yeah, you know me, Jell-O doesn't stand a chance if I have anything to say about it."

"Is this a good thing?"

"Unless you're the Jell-O. I wanted them lined up in tiny shots, so I could mow them down one at a time. I'm not sure they did that or not."

"Probably not."

"I offered to buy a round for the entire floor."

"What did they say?"

"I've learned not to fight back."

A slender woman in a beige business suit stepped into the room. "Mr. Powers, my name is Eddings, Marie Eddings. May I speak with you in the hallway?"

Leland saw Carly slip beneath the covers and pull the sheet over her head.

"The doctors are telling me that this was a close one. Her blood alcohol was hovering near 5 percent."

"She's never lacked for gusto."

"She needs a program of some kind."

"How long can she stay in the hospital?"

"A day, maybe two, but you know hospitals, they like to keep the patients flowing right through."

"So where do I go?"

"I have to believe an in-patient program is the best and the longer the stay, the better."

"How long is long?"

"Ninety days or more. Studies show that the thirty-day ones are less effective, especially for people like Carly."

"And where do I find one of the good ones?"

"We can help you. I've already made some calls. We think the best one is a local nonprofit not too far from here, the Holy Order of Recovered Sisters."

"Is it religious? She may not like that."

"Not really but they do believe in prayer. The founder is Devon Walker. She does a nice job."

§

The old house that he was looking for was sliced in between an aging apartment and a split-level home beyond its prime. In the front yard stood a giant poster painted in red and blue trim, Holy Order of Recovered Sisters—Founded by Devon Walker, 1966.

He mounted the steps but lingered on the porch. Maybe it was just one more incident that he and his ex-wife had to endure. Once Carly got back home and realized she had flirted with the other side, her supreme indulgence in liquor and despair might vanish like a fast-acting rainstorm.

The more he thought about it, the more he liked it, enough so he nearly turned and fled back to the safety of his room and his endless dreams of tomatoes and what it would be like to introduce his road warriors to pure, unadulterated pleasure when he handed them a juicy red fruit he had grown all by himself.

Before he could settle in and fly with his fantasy, the door opened and a scrawny but pleasant-looking woman of twenty-five said, "Can we help you?"

The urge to run was still with him, but he failed to bring forth the courage. "I'm here to see Devon Walker, the hospital sent me."

"Do you have an appointment?"

"No, I didn't think to call, but I've been dinged around pretty good lately and my head isn't on very straight."

"Then you're in the right place."

She held the door and Leland stepped inside. What he saw was a large living room with a couch and three overstuffed chairs. Not far away was a coffee table covered with magazines. *Life*, *Time*, and *Newsweek* all looked like they'd been blazed through more than a few times.

"Have a seat. I'll tell Devon you're here to see her."

Leland nodded.

"And your name?" She asked.

"Leland Powers."

"That's a pretty one."

The woman slipped away and Leland heard the low rumbling sounds of voices coming from a nearby room. He could see three older women setting up chairs and fussing with a coffee pot.

"She can see you now," the pleasant-looking woman said.

Leland followed her through a long hallway to a small office overlooking an alley bulging with garbage cans and run-down cars.

"Devon, Mr. Powers is here to see you."

Leland stepped into her room and was greeted by a small black woman, sporting an accent that made him think of New York City.

"Come in, come in, no need to be bashful around here."

Leland held out his hand and squeezed. The warmth coming into him caused his stomach to flare and a thin trickle of sweat to break out across the back of his neck.

"So you're the one Marie Eddings told me about?"

"One and the same."

"Why don't you fill me in on what's been going on."

"It's my daughter, Carly. She's way in over her head

this time."

"Alcohol?"

"And lots of it."

"What can you tell me about her?"

"Thirty-seven, casino worker, cantankerous as hell and has always had a mind of her own."

"What's her pattern of drinking?"

"There have been spot fires brewing for a long time, dating back to high school. But this last one has turned into a raging forest fire, and I don't know what to do about it."

"How did she land in the hospital?"

"I put her there. I thought she was going to choke to death."

"That has been known to happen. Not everyone is a survivor. I've seen many topple by the wayside. She's lucky you were there."

"I had no choice."

"What can you tell me about yourself, Mr. Powers. Are you married?"

"Used to be but not anymore. Been divorced for less than a year."

"That's no fun. So tell me, what do you do for a living?"

"I run a hotel, the Eleanor, it's not far from here."

"That's a pretty name."

"I guess I never thought about it that way."

Devon went on to bleed into her own tale of woe, how she'd been a singer and veered into parties and stayed too long, and how men prowled the sidelines, some of them finding their way, others there to do nothing more than to leer and pitch their wares. The whole time her New York way of speaking was biting off sentences with sharp angles and cutting corners with rich distinct phrasings. From there she dove into what Carly's life would be like over the next ninety days. Individual counseling and group settings would lead the way. There were to be no visitors or calls for at least nine days. And the hope would always be the same, that Carly's need to swim inside the intoxicating brew of heavy liquor would diminish and the finer version of herself would rise to the top.

"Do we need to talk about money?" Leland asked.

"Our program costs five thousand, less if you're destitute."

"I can handle that."

"And whatever you do, don't give this more thought than it deserves. If you can stay busy, so much the better."

§

For several nights, he rode only in his room. Aspasia and her scrunched-up way of walking was his only thought. He knew that he was nothing and that he had nothing. His room was merely a stopping-off point, a shell with four walls and little else, the alley outside a plume of smoke streaming through the neighborhood. He knew it was time to plant or be planted.

He stood and stared beneath his sink. Down there in the darkness were two trays of tomato seeds. All he yearned for now was the flow of water and the smell of dirt.

Only last week, he had mixed his ingredients with the care of a doctor on a late-night call. He finished off by dropping two seeds into each tiny cup and sprinkling them with water. His only task now was to treat his tomatoes like they were children of his own.

Later the following week, he was on the phone with Carly. Her voice was clear and to the point. "Remember me?"

"Of course."

"Devon said it was all right to make a call."

"How are you getting along with the other women?"

"Let me tell you, there are some real fast-action types here."

"Is that a good thing?"

"If you like pain it is."

"What about Devon? Do you see much of her?"

"Now, there's a woman who has definitely fought with the angry demons. You'd need an army if you wanted to go up against her."

Scream and fury, Leland had to like that.

"She wants me to start thinking about a family day. Mom will come, won't she?"

"You know she will, just tell us when."

"It won't be right away, and it won't be anything fancy. Most likely the three of us will sit on the back porch and drink some herbal tea."

"Herbal tea?"

"Devon says I'm not quite ready for caffeine."

§

And every evening was the same. He'd fill a bottle with water and leave it on the nightstand next to his bed. In the morning, while still in his undershirt, he'd kneel in front of his sink and spray his tiny offerings with a fine mist. Finished, he would lean forward and pat the soil with his fingertips and try placing Aspasia's crippled leg in the center of his mind.

Not long after came visiting day at the Holy Order of Recovered Sisters. Standing on the sidewalk, he spotted Dorothy emerging from her car. Her stride was measured, if not focused, and she walked nearly the entire way before lifting her head and seeing Leland standing there, a fixture of pensiveness.

"This is one thing I thought we'd never be doing," Dorothy said.

"I was hoping it would be different now that she was with Immers."

"We've spent our life hoping she'd change her ways."

Inside they were ushered to the back of the property. The other women, some more hard-bitten than Carly ever was, stared up at them. To them Leland and Dorothy were merely passing through, in no way permanent fixtures; that role was only for those who'd been scorched and abandoned along the way.

Carly was sitting in the sunlight near the fence that ran along the alley. Her smile was serene, and she stood as if the initial meeting had obviously been rehearsed. "Welcome," she said.

She and Dorothy hugged and Leland followed with a hard tug of his own but somehow he pulled it off.

"Have a seat, I think Devon will be joining us in a little while."

And so there they were, the whole of them, puny and divided, held together by the slightest hum of recovery.

"I don't even remember what happened," Carly said.

"I found you."

"Was I at Don's?"

"No, home."

Carly gave the floor a second look. "I try calling him, but his phone has been disconnected."

"I made a few calls of my own. He's been transferred to Vegas."

"For good?"

"Most likely."

"Carly, you need to think about getting better,"

Dorothy said.

"Devon said that she and I are a lot alike. The way we've lived."

"Did she carry cocktails?"

"No, but she was a singer in the Bronx. And let's say she piled up some points."

"How'd she get to Nevada?"

"She woke up one day and said she needed to see the desert, so she bought a ticket and found her way to Pyramid Lake. Cold-stoned drunk the entire way."

"And?" Dorothy asked.

"She lay on the beach and baked."

"That worked?" Leland asked.

"I guess so, she said she was in dreamland most of the time."

"What does it mean?"

"Not sure, but from there she landed in a place like this one, and it's been up ever since."

"So where do we go from here?" Dorothy asked.

"Devon is telling me not to think about it. She said this is what I'm doing and that's all I should be concerned with."

"But this does come to an end, right? You can't live here forever."

"Wouldn't that be nice? It's so quiet, I've come to relish it."

"But don't we need to be realistic?" Dorothy asked.

"I know, but the thought of going back into the clubs and slinging it out every night and collapsing on the couch at night. It's just so hard."

"Maybe it's time to listen to Devon and nothing else," Leland said.

Carly's eyes brightened. "And here's the lady of whom

we speak."

Leland looked up and saw Devon moving their way. She was wearing a bright-red dress and her hair was piled high in a bun.

"Nice to you see all of you today."

Leland stood up and smiled at her, then introduced Dorothy, who in turn nodded in a friendly way.

"Carly's coming right along. Right now we have her in the kitchen. By next week, we'll be assigning her a permanent task."

"I like scrubbing every dish clean."

"This girl's got some grit, that's for sure," Devon said.

"I wonder where she gets that?" Dorothy asked.

Devon let go with a huge laugh and stared right at Leland. "I hear you're all spit and fire. And what's this I hear about a garden on the roof of your hotel?"

"Why not?"

"I'm from the Bronx, we've got plants on the roof, on the balconies, even in the hallways."

"See, nothing wrong with it. Besides, the place needs some freshening up, and a tomato is the only way I know to go about it."

"So what do you plan to do with the fruits of your labor?"

"Give them away, what else?"

"You could sell them and make a few bucks."

"Not me."

"Toss some our way, we'll eat them, won't we Carly?'

"I guess pleasure comes in all forms," Carly said.

"I'll make sure some find their way here."

Devon walked away and Leland put his eyes on her until she wound her way around the corner and disappeared.

"I really like her," Carly said.

"Seems like a dynamo," Dorothy added.

Thoughts of planting tomatoes and spying on Aspasia up in the air played through Leland's mind. So did thoughts of the Holy Order of Recovered Sisters. He had to admit there was no musty odor here. Devon must have swept it away and pushed it down the street where it belonged.

§

Coming out of the low-riding hills of southern Idaho, Leland always had one rule in mind, never throw anything away and his basement bore witness to that decree. Strewn from one end to the other, were old suitcases, boxes of clothes, broken-down nightstands. In the last one were a string of Christmas lights he had tossed aside years ago, and there were strung together in an ugly mess. After all, this was the Eleanor Hotel, where chaos hummed below the surface on most days.

Today's attempt to find something he needed to do pertained to several strings of Christmas lights he had thrown into a box some time ago. He knew if he kept pressing, they'd turn up at some point.

In the rear of the basement, he spotted three large boxes, and he tore into each one of them with the same brewing vengeance he did most things, something just shy of an all-out assault. And to his credit, he did find what he was looking for. The Christmas lights were in the last box he ripped into, and he discovered they were all strung together in one ugly mess. After all, this was the Eleanor Hotel, where chaos hummed below the surface on most days.

But that didn't matter much to him one way or the other. What did were his juicy red tomatoes, and that's what had him in a dither since waking up around 3:30 that morning. Last night the weatherman said that a cold front was moving in from Canada and that it would be wise for everyone to protect their vegetables. That's all it took for him to get worked up into a tizzy, so even before the sun bled through the clouds, he was on the roof wrapping each one of his many plants with sheets of plastic and tying them into off with heavy swaths of the toughest tape he could lay his hands on. After that he grabbed his hose and cut loose with a swath of water that was so wide and wonderful that he soaked his garden until it was about five ticks shy of being a muddy mess, but not so messy he was afraid to wind his Christmas lights around the base of every one of his plants.

And that's what he did next, hoping that the lights would generate enough heat that it might make the difference between having a bunch of frozen little nubs of fruit as opposed to big tasty ones that with a little luck might open someone's mind up so wide that they'd see the world in a whole new way.

On the rooftop he strung three strings of lights out before him and went to work on the knots. Every now and then he'd have to stop and blow on the tips of his fingers to keep them from freezing, but after another hour or so, he scored another victory in his need to munch his way through life nearly undeterred.

He tied the lines together and ran them through the garden in a long, circular path. Finished, and nearly so frozen that he yearned for a vat of anything hot, he raced downstairs and rummaged for an extension cord, which he found hiding underneath the back steps. Knowing his own brand of Judgment Day was upon him, he raced back upstairs and plugged the cord into the outlet next to the door leading into the storage room. And outside he saw what he needed to see: a bunch of plants wrapped up like mummies with what looked like tiny little diamonds burning at their feet. And he was so happy, he did a little dance, hoping he had mustered enough courage to put one over on Mother Nature, quite possibly the best friend he'd ever had in this life.

§

After bailing off the roof and turning the fate of his little red wonderments over to whomever you're supposed to turn things over to, Leland hightailed it over to Carly's for another showdown with Dorothy about the future as it pertained to their daughter. The trouble was, Leland no more understood the future than he did the origins of a kumquat.

About a block from his destination, he slowed his pickup and began sizing up the Highlands, the hijackers of his daughter's life, or so he liked to believe. He didn't know how many times he had laid awake at night, even before he landed in the back room at the Eleanor, and blamed those damn clubs for being the ruination of his daughter's life. Maybe if she'd gone to work for the power company, she would have been fine, or maybe she'd been the one with a bottle of rum tucked away in her bottom drawer and known to do the hula out in the hallway when no one was watching.

To his surprise his former wife was already standing in the parking lot. He stepped out of his pickup at the same time Dorothy rubbed her gloved hands together in a futile attempt to keep warm.

"Who saw this weather coming?" she said.

"Not me, for sure."

"I woke up thinking about your tomato plants. Do you think they'll survive this?"

"They better. I've been up since four wrapping them in plastic and running Christmas lights throughout the bed."

"Christmas lights?"

"They generate warmth, that's all I know."

Dorothy shook her head. "We shall not be denied. Isn't that how it goes with you?"

"What was I supposed to do, let them freeze?"

"No, that wouldn't be right."

"Let's get inside, the landlord should be coming right along."

"Harlan said we'd cover this month's rent, seeing how you did the first one."

It took some doing but Leland said, "Tell him thank you."

Inside Carly's place was the same, classy but stilled, but now the air was stale and Leland swore he smelled the odor of that terrible day when Carly flirted with the other side of life.

They walked into the bedroom and saw that nothing had changed. The bed was still unmade, and a half-filled wine goblet sat on the nightstand. Not far away Carly's casino outfit was strewn across the only chair in the room. The only noticeable difference was the window was now new and shiny, seeing how Leland had hired a company to come over and fix the darn thing.

"So what do we think we're going to do here? Is she going to move back in and pretend nothing happened?" Dorothy asked.

"I have no idea. I just hope Devon can spin some magic with her."

"I have to say I don't agree with this only-for-today philosophy that those types of people talk about so much.

I thought we're supposed to plan for the future."

"I gave up trying to figure this whole thing out some time ago."

"We can't be thinking like that either."

"I hope I never see her like that again."

There was a knock on the door and Leland yelled, "Come in."

In walked Mr. Looway, the perennial keeper of the monthly rent, the very same commodity that Leland had been known to relish.

"How is Carly? Is she feeling better?"

"We saw her the other day, she seems to be coming along," Dorothy said.

"Everyone is rooting for her. She's always been well-liked around here."

"She once told me this place is a nonstop party, is that true?" Leland asked.

Mr. Looway, a squat man with a square head said, "I like to think of it as controlled chaos."

Leland took three steps closer to him and sized him up. "Did you ever think of trying to rein them in? Maybe if you'd applied a little pressure, a lot of them would have never crossed the line."

"Excuse me?"

"You heard me."

"These maniacs are nonstop and were long before I ever met up with them. I do my best to keep them in bounds."

"We know how well that worked out."

"Leland, please, not now," Dorothy said.

Leland accepted the command and walked away. In the kitchen he opened a cupboard and pretended that Mr. Looway wasn't standing in the living room.

"I wish you two well, but I need to get going," Mr. Looway said, opening the door and stepping outside.

"That was more than a little rude," Dorothy said.

"Well, it's true, isn't it? Maybe if he'd put the clamps to Carly, we wouldn't be in this mess."

"How good are you at keeping your troops in line?"

"That's different, they're already broken."

§

With Carly riding high in the misty fumes of a pink cloud recovery, Leland was able to return to the land. He'd water by day and weed and wonder by night. Rolling through the growing season, he finally saw evidence that he was every bit the farmer that his brother had proved to be throughout his life.

By early fall small balls of fruit began forming on the vines. Each one was small and green and hard to the touch. In his freest moments, he would offer his thanks to every one of his plants. Occasionally he would try to conjure up Aspasia but she never came to him. His day-to-day included only the soil and the water needed to keep the plants going.

Later in the fall, he spent one afternoon cleaning the fingerprints off his front window. To his surprise, he saw Carly and Devon coming down the street. His daughter appeared bright and cheery, wearing a pair of jeans and a white T-shirt. Devon, a diehard of her East Coast up-bringing, was in full display of color, a yellow blouse and satiny blue slacks that hung over the tops of red and white clogs in two even lines.

"We thought we'd surprise you," Carly said, gliding through the doorway.

"I told her I had to see this place called the Eleanor and sure enough this is it."

"Forty-nine rooms of dislocated people, but who's counting," Carly said.

Leland sat his can of Windex on the coffee table next to the front window. "I didn't know walks were part of the deal."

"They are when you're doing as well as this one," Devon said.

"I now head up the cleaning crew."

"Head it up, girl, you *are* the cleaning crew. None of the others can even come close to your mastery."

"I'm tired of dirt."

"Kind of like the smell here, huh?" Leland said.

A puzzled look formed on Carly's face. "But I haven't disrespected anyone in the process."

"I've heard this more than a few times," Devon said. "So you went on a crusade about some mysterious musty odor that was driving you crazy."

"Nothing mysterious about it whatsoever, it's all around us."

Devon sniffed the air like a little dog on the prowl. "You know, you might be on to something there. Besides, how cool is that, freeing the world of a musty smell."

"So far the mustiness is winning out."

"But you gotta like a man who can get after it," Devon said.

"I get after mine with a toothbrush," Carly said.

"And does she ever. I caught her the other day with her butt up in the air and digging into the corners under the sink with a ratty old toothbrush. I said, oh my Lord, there ain't no stop in this girl whatsoever."

"Sometimes dirt needs to know who's in charge," Carly said.

"I hear that," Devon said.

Leland wanted to know about the wine and whiskey, but he knew better than to ask.

"What's this I hear about a rooftop garden?" Devon asked.

"Right up there," Leland said, pointing up to the ceiling.

"The first time I heard her going on about it, I thought maybe she was headed around the bend. You know we see that sometimes, and that's when we know the girls have to have some real help."

"Let's take a ride," Leland said.

The three of them slipped into the elevator and rode to the top. Devon shook her head. "Where'd you get this thing? They must have flown it in from Siberia."

"The hotel was built in 1926. In those days, it was a luxury."

Stepping outside, Leland said, "There it is, one man's tomato garden."

And there it was, a patch of soil paying homage to rows of tomato plants growing wild and free not far from the turbulent casinos up the street. Each was tied to a tall wooden stake that Leland had driven into the ground with the one and only hammer he owed.

"They're close to being ready," Leland said.

"I think they're beautiful. And you did this by yourself?" Devon asked.

"Me and only me."

"Now, that's what I call impressive. Whew! How many trips up and down the steps did you have to make?"

"I stopped counting after the first backache."

"Ache! My back would have snapped."

Leland beamed like he hadn't beamed for a long time. "Here, have one, they're ready to be picked."

Carly stared at Devon like they were about ready to step out of an airplane and plunge to their deaths.

"Go on, help yourself, there's plenty for everyone," Leland said.

Devon went first, grabbing the first and firmest one she could find. She held it in her hand and gripped it like a baseball. "Nice, nice, I'm gonna have it with dinner tonight."

Carly bobbed up and down like it was one of the bigger decisions she'd ever have to make.

Devon cleared her throat and spoke right up. "Come on, girl, we don't have forever. Pick one, and we'll get going."

Carly sized them up before picking one of the smaller ones near the bottom of the vine, not far from her feet. "Now what?"

"Take it home and eat the damn things," Leland said.

Carly slid to the side and looked like she was brewing for a fight.

Devon stepped up and put her peacemaking skills out there for both of them to see. "Come on, let's go, we need to get back to the ranch. We've got a new girl coming in this afternoon."

"Speaking of the ranch, aren't we coming up on the ninety-day mark?" Leland asked.

Carly nodded, but Devon spoke right up. "We're thinking of extending her stay for another two weeks. We still have some work to do."

"If you think that's best," Leland said.

"We need to figure out the next step, like where Carly is going to live and work."

Carly let go with a big sigh but didn't say anything.

"I'm sure you could stay with Dorothy and Harlan if

you needed to," Leland said.

"We'll pass on that one," Carly said, shaking her head.

"What about a job? Do you think you could get back on at the ShowCase?"

"Unlikely."

"What if we got ahold of Don and ask him to make a few phone calls?"

"I don't want to go back into the clubs."

"Those places blow my mind. I look around and I think toxicity with a capital T. Make that two capital Ts," said Devon.

"But what are you going to do for money?"

"I wouldn't mind working in a flower shop."

Leland gulped. He couldn't see his easily frustrated daughter working in a shop surrounded by lilies and having to water a bunch of little pots. "Do you know what they pay?"

"Probably not much."

Devon stepped it up a notch. "We don't have to answer any of these questions right now. That's what the sisterhood is for."

Leland knew better than to argue. Instead the three of them took the elevator down to the first floor. Devon stood near the counter and gave the place the once-over. "I swear, you've got the voodoo working here, baby."

§

Leland woke with only Carly and Devon on his mind, though he knew his upcoming ritual was meant for him and only him. Last night he had given his garden a well-meaning run-through by plucking one juicy tomato off the vine and slicing it into four pieces while he sat on the end of his bed and hoped that his taste buds would light up with the joy that only rooftop vegetables can provide. And sure enough, they did. Every bite allowed him to sink more deeply into himself and be grateful for the many trips up and down the back steps with a bucketful of dirt in each hand.

That morning on the roof he plunged into his bevy of red fruit and began picking them one by one and filling up an old wicker basket that he had bought recently at a thrift shop for less than three dollars.

By the time he finished, he must have plucked sixteen or seventeen large-sized tomatoes off the vine before making his way to the second floor. There he had a well-thought-out plan to help every one of his long-term tenants, and he didn't need a chart this time.

First up was Mr. Logan, a retiree who holed up in his room a good twenty hours a day and didn't speak to anyone but Leland. Luckily after a few raps on the door, he could hear the rustling of feet and a gruff cough or two.

Finally the door opened and Leland went into his spiel right away. "Mr. Logan, I have something for you."

"What is it?"

"It's a tomato that I grew up on the roof."

"So."

"I was thinking you might like to have one."

"What am I supposed to do with it?"

"Eat it."

"Why?"

"Because it's good for you."

"Says who?"

"Says anyone who knows anything about soil and sun."

"So what's wrong with what I eat?"

"Nothing, but I want you to experience something better."

"Why?'

"Because it's better, that's how life works. We always want something better than what we have."

"I'm okay just the way I am.""

"Just take the damn thing and eat it. What's the harm in that?"

"If it will make you happy, I'll eat it, but I really don't need the intrusion."

"Trust me, you might even enjoy it."

Next up was a line cook with a passion for cards and women who were always a step or two beyond his reach. Leland knocked on his door and went to work right away about the gloriousness of eating from one's own garden. His weary tenant listened with full intent, then reached out and grabbed the tomato before Leland had a chance to finish selling him on his plan to make his hotel a better place to live in. In fact he closed the door so fast, he nearly clipped Leland's nose in the process. Leland shook his head and realized he was going to have to retool his plan if he was going to resurrect the diets of his misdirected tenants.

From there was a swath of rooms he wasn't going to bother with. They belonged to the over-nighters, and enriching them with culinary delight was beyond his scope of influence. Someone in California or elsewhere was going to have to step up and guide them to the Promised Land.

On the top floor, he wasted no time in knocking on Mrs. Dauer's door and hoping he could pull her into the forefront of his nutritional plan. If he could do that, many of the other guests might trail right along, and then Leland could spend the rest of the fall basking in the delight of his garden and knowing that he had created an oasis right there amid the clanging world of slot machines and the loud scream of men calling dice.

Mrs. Dauer answered on the third knock and there she stood, beady-eyed and defiant, backed over both shoulders by the old familiar room she had lived in all these years.

"Here, I have some tomatoes for you."

"What are you trying to do, poison me?"

"Nothing of the kind. I'm just trying to help people feel better about themselves."

"Everyone knows you want me out of here, that's why you upended my room not long ago."

"I was simply yearning for a cleaner place for all of us to live in. Nothing more than that."

"Why don't you dummy up and go for the money, that's what most people like you do."

"There's gotta be more to it than that. Now, do you want the tomatoes or not?"

Mrs. Dauer laid her eyes on them like she could see the inner beings of each and every one of them. "Are you sure you're not trying to do me in?"

"Trust me, I'm a guy who wants to pass his tomatoes around the hotel, nothing more than that."

"Well, none of us here think of you as a liar."

With that Mrs. Dauer accepted her pieces of fruit with no mention of making it a peace offering. After all, a tomato was only a tomato.

Walking down the steps, Leland felt a bit betrayed. He knew now it was going to take some time for his magical seeds to work their wonderment. For now he had to keep tilling the soil.

§

Leland had a plan all planned out and it didn't involve any sweat or grime. He was going to buy the evening paper and read it from page one all the way through. The rest of his time would be devoted to sorting out what to do with Carly when it was time for her to come home.

To his delight O'Dell's Fine Foods and Even Better Groceries wasn't very busy, a few college kids and an old man with a cane, so grabbing a newspaper was easy. A small item in the middle of the page caught his attention right away. The United States and Britain were working to launch the Copernicus Satellite in an effort to view certain aspects of the sky in ultraviolet light. Leland nodded and smiled at what he was about to read.

Stepping in line he spotted Mr. Logan already at the counter. He was buying two cans of hair spray and a large-sized can of tomatoes. Leland couldn't help but tap him on the shoulder and lean into him. "Why are you buying that damn thing?"

"Because I need it."

"But I just gave you a tomato fresh off the roof, and there's plenty more when you're ready."

Mr. Logan turned and faced his holier-than-thou landlord. "I need it because it's long-lasting."

"So is death."

"What's that supposed to mean?"

"Do you know that can of tomatoes is chock-full of sodium?"

"So? I plan to tuck it away in my sock drawer. Who knows, I might need to heat it up someday."

"But I gave you a tomato."

"I don't want fresh, I want longevity. Besides, the one you gave me went soft inside after a few days."

"You weren't supposed to stare at it, you were supposed to eat it."

"I didn't feel like eating it. I wanted to make sure it was real first."

Mr. Logan tucked his bag close to his body and walked out the door.

"Putz," Leland said.

§

But he did not let sodium get in his way. Every morning he'd stand in his lobby and hand out tomatoes like they were nothing more than bags of candy. Most of his down-on-their-luck guests accepted his offering in a friendly way but walked away frazzled and begotten. To his delight some smiled and feigned interest in wanting to improve their deeply abused way of eating. Leland even went so far as to boil some soup one evening and leave a bowl brewing on the back table. By the end of the day, it was only half full, and Leland felt a stream of nobility pass through his veins like he had never experienced. His most important undertaking was running a basketful over to Devon and leaving it on the front desk. Later in the day, he received a call that opened with "Thank you for your green thumb," and he swam lovingly in what felt like a warm and certainly welcomed way of living.

A few days later, his maverick high ran amuck. It happened one morning as he tried to find his way through his monthly numbers. After an hour of pulling on his adding machine, he had a ream of paper flowing off the counter, and his figures weren't even close to coinciding.

"What the . . ."

No matter how many times he tried, he kept coming up $8.50 short and closing out the month without his figures being in balance was paramount to walking outside without any clothes on.

After grousing for a good five minutes, he knew the problem. It was Carly and knowing what to do with her after she stopped hiding out at the Holy Order of

Recovered Sisters.

"Damn numbers, it's getting so I couldn't care less."

He threw his pencil across the floor and walked outside. The sidewalk was flowing with people, some short and straggling, others in business attire with pale, placid faces. He leaned on the side of his own building and ran down his options for what to do with Carly. Without a doubt, the clubs were a bleak one, way too much smoke and way too many Morse Philipses on the prowl. Living with Dorothy and Harlan was bound to be short-lived, if anything at all. He knew there was only one answer and that was to draw her close to him and hope she would start clinging to him instead of taking up residency at the next pool party at the Highland Apartments.

Inside he dialed Devon's number from memory. On the third ring, he was told his call was being transferred.

"And how's the farmer doing today?" she asked.

"Still looking for answers I can't find."

"What did I tell you about that?"

Leland tried pulling her mandate up to the surface but had little success. "I was wondering if I could sit down with you and Carly later today and discuss what the next step is going to be?"

"Consider it a done deal."

Later that afternoon, Leland walked into Devon's office and plopped down right in front of her. She greeted him with a two-handed handshake and a warm smile. "I've been mulling this over, and maybe I've come up with a solution about how Carly can earn a living."

"Let's have her come in and see what she has to say. After all, we need to think of something this week. We have a new girl coming into the program and she's going to be living in Carly's room."

Carly walked in with the smell of Comet about her. "This is a surprise."

"I stopped by to run something by the two of you."

"Let's hear it," Devon said.

"I think you're right about the ShowCase or any of those places. They've been known to wear on the best of people."

Carly squirmed in her seat. "I called a few flower shops but with no luck. I guess I'll have to put another fantasy to sleep."

"Now, Carly, let's stay positive," Devon said.

"Why don't you come work for me at the Eleanor?"

"I'm not a farmer."

"And I'm not here to talk about tomatoes."

"Speaking of them, we could use some more," Devon said.

Leland smiled and went on to say, "I mean behind the desk, learning the business."

"You mean, be a clerk?"

"That and some more. Maybe I'm talking about taking on the full operation. Doing the bookwork, hiring and firing if necessary."

"Would that involve evicting people? That could be a trigger," Devon said.

"There's never been much of that."

"And what are you going to be doing?" Carly asked.

"I want to step back a little bit. Doing bookwork isn't what it used to be, and anyway, the way the tomatoes were received, I'm not exactly feeling rejuvenated in the way I was hoping."

"Is your health all right?" Devon asked.

"I hope you're not getting weird again like you were when Mom moved out of the house," Carly said.

"I'm tired of manning the desk nearly every day. Besides, I might tackle the smell again. I never said I was finished with that."

Carly blinked and stared out the window.

"This is a lot to consider. We'll need to process it. We're not about to set Carly up to fail," Devon said.

"I'll need to ponder this," Carly said.

"It might be time for me to do a little global thinking," Leland said.

§

"I've talked to Mom and I'm going to stay with her and Harlan for a few days, maybe a week, and then I'll be ready to work for you."

"We'll go easy at first, maybe a few hours a day."

And with that Leland set about transferring his knowledge of the hotel to pen and paper. He drew up price codes and listed each room and what days rooms went for this and what days they went for that. What came next was information about the maid and who liked towels and who didn't want any. Then there was the way the place was warmed. First one floor, then the other, always careful never to overheat anyone or anything, especially Leland's bag of money.

At night he rehearsed his soliloquies about rent and who could be believed and who had to be dismissed with the pitch of a hard glare. But most of all he worked on his hard-earned wisdom born out of his Mormon heritage about who could stay and who had to go. Seldom was anyone ever asked to leave, only to moderate the way they were acting. He lived by the credo that empty rooms brought in no money. Those misbehavers were there to throw a few dollars his way, enough to make a difference whether a month was dipping into the red or falling into the black.

In only a few days after agreeing to succumb to the gritty charms of the Eleanor, Carly made her debut, not in the full regalia of her old life of wigs and cars and tons of costume jewelry but in the simple attire of tan slacks and a beige blouse. Of course the big question lingered in the air: Could she and her father bond at the level of the hip?

Her first day was nothing more than a drill. Leland sat her down and ran through every figure and theory and philosophy in his own way. Carly tried listening like she never had before, clinging to every word as they dribbled off of his tongue.

"But how am I going to live on what you pay people? I'll have to save up just to get my nails done."

"No one tips, that's for sure. You might have to scale down and get a different car."

Carly in a Ford Maverick, neither she nor her father could see it. Her El Dorado was her pledge to life, liberty, and fancy clothes.

"What was the first night like back at home?" Leland asked.

"Quiet. I sat on the couch and watched TV. The whole time I heard Devon's voice singing in my head. Do this, don't do that, most of all remember to stay in the moment."

"She seems to know her stuff."

"Who's kidding who, she nearly saved my life."

"Try and relax. This place runs close to the edge, but it does all right. In time we'll talk about making you a partner and then you can have a piece of the pie."

"Is there enough to go around?"

"The way I live, there will be."

"I'm tired of walking around scared."

"You'll have to stay close to the Holy Order."

Carly breathed deep and nodded. "Absolutely. In fact, I'm going to a meeting this evening and hope to do so three times a week. Plus, I meet with Devon every Friday afternoon."

§

With the clouds hanging in and the slightest mingling of frost lining the edges of his garden, he knew it was time to put his farmland to rest. He raked up the leaves and a scattering of broken vines and crammed them all into plastic bags and hauled them down the back steps and loaded them onto his pickup.

His adventure with tilling the soil had been a telling one. No doubt he'd had his falling-outs with Logan and Dauer, but it wasn't bleak across the board. A few of his guests thanked him by offering up smiles and some even patted him on the back. His biggest payoff came in the form of a big hallelujah call from Devon not long after he had plopped a basketful of tomatoes on her desk without even asking her permission. Her mention of his green thumb sent him spinning up the ladder of happiness, where he spent the rest of the day swimming in the sound of her warm and luxurious voice.

One day he told Carly that she could take off early, which she did without a lot of fuss or worry when she hightailed it out the door. He smiled and turned his attention to the long columns that Carly had penciled into place in his ledger book sitting right in front of him on the counter. He had to admit that she seemed to have a knack for numbers, maybe something in his genes that had passed onto her.

Also there was her ease of saying, "Yes ma'am" and "No sir," which seemed to come naturally, much to

Leland's delight. Of course, he knew she was held together because of her near-daily visits with Devon and the rest of the sisters who were on the road to recovery.

He worked through the day tidying up the clutter behind his desk and mopping out the back bathrooms, only to see the Holy Grail herself, Devon Walker, walking in the door dressed in Levi's and a white shirt that read "I'm No Angel."

"Leland, how's it going?"

"Pretty good. I sent the wild one home today thinking she could use some time to herself."

"I'm on errands and I thought I'd stop in and say hello. This is the first of a few days off for me."

"I didn't know people like you took time off."

"I'm not like you. I can't dredge it up from the bottom of my being every day of the week like you can."

"I'm hoping Carly hasn't been too much to handle."

"Getting out of those damn casinos was the best thing she ever did. Now all she needs to do is find her way, which she'll do in due time."

"I'll give her a hand. It's not like money is flying out the door these days."

"I understand you live upstairs, is that right?"

"I need to stay close to the action, if you know what I mean."

Devon let go with a big laugh. "She says you don't even have a bath in your own room."

"It's just outside the door, what's wrong with that?"

"Man, that's strong."

"I'm doing a lot better than I was a year ago."

"Being a farmer must help."

"Soil and breath is what it's all about."

"A man with a plan, that's what I say."

Devon leaned into him, enough so her knee grazed across the inside of Leland's thigh. "I'm not exactly adhering to the rule book, but I wouldn't mind seeing where you hole up at night, if you know what I mean."

Leland gazed into her round friendly face until it nearly pushed him sideways. Rubbing up against her would be sheer delight, provided he remembered how to do it.

"It's only a short hop up the steps and down the hallway."

"I'm game if you are," she said.

He slipped his hand into his pocket and handed his room key to Devon. "The four o'clock man should be coming right along."

Devon caressed the key and slipped up the staircase without saying another word. Leland stood there and tried shaking all the muck and mire that had settled into his veins over the years. He told himself a wave was coming and it was best to let it happen.

§

Leland walked into the room and found it dark and cozy, with only the floor lamp in the corner turned on. Devon was lying in the middle of his bed staring up at the ceiling with a soft smile on her face.

"Hey, you," she said. Leland sat on the end of the bed and slipped out of his coat and tie and everything else. Staring at himself, he was embarrassed by the roundness of his belly and the whiteness of his skin. The best he had to offer was the slightest trace of a tan line running across his neck and forearms.

"Who would have thought we would end up here," Devon said.

"Never crossed my mind."

He slid beneath the covers and let it happen, her soft,

serene touch and the slight upturn of her small, firm breasts. Once, twice, even three times, it was white on black and black the other way around, melting and soothing throughout the evening.

By morning a stream of light came into his room. Leland lay there pretending this was his one and only moment in life and he never wanted to budge. But it was Devon who threw back the twisted pile of blankets and walked to the sink and smiled at her reflection in a mirror that long ago clouded with age.

"You know I'm not supposed to be doing this. Clients and staff and never shall the two snuggle between the sheets. I'm not sure what I'll do if anyone finds out."

"Who's going to tell them?"

"Secrets don't last forever."

"We'll blame it on the tomatoes."

"I hear that."

§

One night led to another and another, and it wasn't until Friday evening that Leland was back in his room by himself and resting up from a free fall of erotic delight. Not even Aspasia and all her splendor had surged so deeply into his body and opened up the avenues of his ecstatic wonderment. Everywhere he looked he was right there with it. The sink gleamed a bright friendly white and the slight rip in the shade gave it a sense of dignity and foreboding.

In the morning the hallway carpet was soft and tender beneath his feet and the slight cough behind the many closed doors made him glad he was living with the very people who had made him a small-town businessman with success on his side.

In the lobby he knew that gossip would be the thrill of the day. There'd been way too many squeaks and hollers seeping into the air for them not to have noticed. But Leland surmised that many of his lobby dwellers needed the nastiness of him and Devon to lubricate their minds and give their imaginations a spark to liven up their days.

Carly was standing behind the desk with her shoulders scrunched and her arms folded across her chest.

"How are you getting along this morning?" Leland asked. Carly let go with barely a mumble.

"Are you okay? Did you sleep well last night?" He asked.

"Apparently not as well as you."

Leland's mind flashed with something to say but nothing came to the forefront.

"Is this how I'm supposed to find out, with a bunch of guests gossiping in my ear?"

"It just sort of happened."

"So she just mysteriously ended up in your bed?"

"She stopped by the other day to see you and we got to talking, and the next thing I knew we were upstairs."

"Yeah, for three days."

"Something like that."

"But she's in charge of my recovery."

"We've already talked about it."

"And?"

"All I know is it's been a long haul since your mother left."

Carly stared down at the floor. "But I thought she liked me."

"She does. She thinks you're wonderful."

"I scrubbed her toilets, isn't that enough?"

"It does a person good."

Late in the day, the phone rang and it was Devon on the line. "Carly was just here, and let me tell you, she's one pissed-off little girl."

"I tried talking to her."

"So did I, but she's about to flip her wig."

"There's no reasoning with her when she's like this."

"I hope she doesn't start drinking again."

Leland pondered another day standing by her bed and watching her gurgle what could easily be her last breath. "I told her to go home and get some rest."

"If the other girls find out what happened, this place could blow sideways."

"How come we have to ask permission?"

"That's the wonderful world of theory. Me, I'm living with thunder and rain hanging right over my head."

"Am I ever going to see you again?"

A long pause hit the line. "Sure was nice. Something very sexy about the way you do things."

"You mean having a hotel?"

"Man, I don't care about that. I'm talking about your inner beat, the one you've been chasing for a while."

"More like it's been chasing me."

§

By 4:30 Leland was up and out of bed. It had been one of those nights of tossing and turning, even cussing along the way. He couldn't help but think his three days of romping and stomping with Devon was nothing more than a slice of cosmic delight he might never taste again.

Over coffee he decided it was time to get back to soldiering through the day, one foot in front of the other but he feared he'd never see Devon again. But to his delight, his phone rang that night and he heard the soft purr of her voice filling up his ear. "I've been on the phone with Carly most of the day, and she's still burning with anger."

"Did she drink?" Leland asked.

"Not yet, but you can bet your Eleanor Hotel that she's been thinking about it."

"She has to know there's no turning back the clock."

"Yeah, but I'm not a chick who tears things apart. I'm the kind that puts them back together. Or at least that's how I think I am."

"So what are we going to do?"

"I told her the three of us need to sit down and have a little talk. How about stopping by after you get off work?"

"What's that going to be like?"

"Prepare to go deep, that's all I know to say."

§

Leland hung up and stared at the switchboard. Feeling he'd rather get kicked in the face by a mule than discuss why he wanted to wake up alongside Devon every morning of every day. Nonetheless, he knew there was no use fighting with the both of them. Devon was a search-through-the-problems kind of person, and he was hoping that Carly was on her way to being the same way. But he was the type that like to hide out and pretend that everything was all right.

At four he took off running for the Holy Order, where he was led right away into a room where Devon was sitting behind a desk with a crimped face and a nervous look in her eye. Carly was right in front of her and acting like she'd been hauled off the playground and scolded for swinging too high on a swing set.

"Now, we need to remember that we're simply three friends talking through some things that went sideways on us," Devon said.

"It feels like I've been betrayed by the only two people

I can trust," Carly said.

"We are here to help you," Devon said.

"First it's the house, then the smell, then it's tomatoes that are the gift of God, when in fact they're nothing more than a bunch of tomatoes."

Leland hated hearing his tomatoes being defiled by an angry drunk, even if it was his daughter.

"Carly, feeling betrayed is the thing to do, because you were, and I'm the one who played dipsy-doodle with the rules, the very same ones I helped write. But it just happened, Carly, no one was planning it."

"You think it's easy sitting in that lobby and listening to everyone snicker about what was going on upstairs?"

"I've tried my best here, but with Harlan whisking your mother away and me selling the house and everything you've been through, there were times when I wasn't sure if you were going to make it," Leland said.

"I wasn't that bad," Carly said.

"Carly, you were in pretty sad shape, let's not deny that."

"Look, I'm not a prude, but this is a lot to come to terms with."

"Maybe you're going to have a new family," Devon said.

"What does that mean?"

"I'm not sure, but for now, everything is on hold."

"Are you saying it was nothing more than a one-night stand? Carly asked.

"Actually, it was three nights," Leland said.

"What I'm saying is that for right now, there aren't going to be any more shenanigans," Devon said.

Leland could have cussed right there on the spot but he kept his mouth wired shut.

"Your recovery is important to us. This is what we do, we're professionals here," Devon said.

Carly shrugged. "Who hasn't had a one-night stand?"

"I need a glass of water," Leland said.

§

Leland went home and felt sorry for himself. Even the thought of his rooftop garden was irritating. Late one evening, about two days after the big sit-down with Carly, the phone rang. It was Devon's voice lighting up the airwaves.

"I can't stand this, I need to come over."

"What about Carly?"

"We can't cater to every one of her needs. Besides, I miss that little room of yours."

So Devon came back and they did what they did oh so well, they heated up the sheets and let the moans and groans ring throughout the hotel. After one vigorous romp slightly before dawn, Leland lay on his back and stroked Devon's neck and shoulders. She responded by rubbing his chest and letting go with a big sigh. "That was one of the longest couple of days of my life."

"I was beginning to think we were done for."

"I sat at work and couldn't wrap my mind around a damn thing. All I could think about was this room."

"It's cozy, isn't it."

"So what do we tell Carly?" Devon asked.

"When it comes to her, I'm way in over my head."

"I guess I have no choice. I'll tell her I'm a damn liar."

"No telling what's she going to say."

"I run a clean shop over there. I've never once come close to crossing the line. Until now, that is."

Leland coughed but didn't say anything.

"You know, Carly is no mystery to me. I am her and

she is me. We're sisters fighting this thing together."

"She might come around."

"Over there we talk all the time about living your life the right way."

"So where did you come to learn all this?"

"Leland, I'm trying to tell you. I'm not all bouquets and pretty flowers. I've been down the road in more ways than one."

Leland rolled onto his side and Devon was right there with him.

"I was in a band and we were good, I mean good."

"Is that right?"

"We were Devon Walker and the Pearly Gates, and we played all the time. We even flirted with a record deal in LA."

"So what happened?"

"I'm what happened. We had a three-week gig here in Reno in a place called the Nut Grove. The idea was to get in good shape and then head for the studio in Los Angeles and show them what we had. And brother, we had it going."

"And?"

"Three shows a night and a bunch of dry air, that's what happened. I ended up tearing my throat to shreds. One doctor told me to take a year off and try not to put any strain on my vocal cords."

"Did you?"

"Are you kidding me? I decided to stay drunk and sing my ass off. No way I was turning my back on a record deal."

"Did you ever get to LA?"

"I let it all hang out. I got warm and toasty before every set and I leaned into that mic, let me tell you, I was shrieking like a banshee."

"And that's when it went crazy?"

"I woke up one morning, and I could barely speak above a whisper."

"So how did Pyramid Lake come into the picture?"

"I didn't find it, it found me. I passed out on the couch in this little bungalow we were renting and I had a dream."

"That's when you saw the water and the beach?"

"I'm telling you I saw the pyramids, up close and personal, and I had never even heard of the place. Man, I'm from the Bronx, what do I know about Pyramid Lake?"

Leland sat up on the bed and reached for his T-shirt.

"I crawled off the couch and borrowed a car and that was it. I laid on the beach and sobered up."

"And it's been up ever since?"

"I felt like I was burning in hell, but let me tell you, my dream life scorched into me with guns a blazing. For three weeks after that, I saw tomorrow. I'd have a dream and the next day it would come true. It was some sort of freaky but it was real, that much I know."

"Sounds brutal."

"I mean, that lake left an imprint on me. Luckily I stumbled into a recovery center a lot like the Holy Order."

"And now you're the one in charge."

"Let's hope this little maneuver doesn't cost me my job."

"I don't think she'll go ballistic."

"For now I better come and go by the back door."

"That's not how I like to think of things."

"Trust me, that back-of-the-bus bullshit is in my DNA."

§

The next day the phone rang and somehow Leland knew it was Devon.

"I don't have what it takes."

"What are you talking about?"

"I was going to call Carly and tell her what's been going on but I chickened out."

"Maybe I should try and talk to her."

"I don't see that happening. She's still pretty delicate."

"So what do you think I should do?"

"Why don't you come over to my house? That way I don't have to slink around like I'm running from the police."

"I guess that would work."

Devon ran down the who, what, where, and when of how to find her place and with a cool whispery send-off, said see you later. Behind the wheel, he wondered if he were headed back to the suburbs and a house ten times bigger than the place he now lived in, complete with a backyard and a newspaper showing in the driveway of every house up and down the street.

After a few turns and a long stretch of neighborhood homes, Leland rolled up in front of Devon's and parked behind her '72 Datsun, still shiny and undoubtedly fresh off the showroom floor. He climbed out of his pickup, walked up to the door and stared at the two-bedroom home with the tile roof and red brick chimney.

"My man, come on in."

Leland stepped inside and was greeted with a huge hug and a light kiss on the cheek.

"Now we have some room to roam, if you know what I mean," Devon said.

From there Leland stepped into the aroma of what smelled like chicken and green beans.

"I got this recipe from my grandmother."

"Smells like something I haven't had in a long time."

"Maybe the sequestered life is coming to a close."

Leland responded with a big gulp and little else.

"Let me show you what I call home."

From room to room, it was hardwood floors and fancy rugs in various shapes and sizes. One room was a small den with a TV that sat on top of a dresser. Next to it was a shelf of books with titles like *Feel Better Now* and *Learning How to Let Go*. On the walls were photos of Devon and her many bands. Names like the Soul Busters and Three Brothers and a Sister and of course the Pearly Gates.

"So that's the group that almost made you famous."

"I ought to rename it the Band Who Could Have Been."

Leland took a closer look and didn't know what to say. Afros, bellbottoms, and a smile or two, and a whole lot of hard, angry stares, the kind that only an artist can muster up.

"Ever think about singing again?"

Devon shook her head. "Not me, not even in the shower. Pyramid Lake told me to let it be, and let it be I did. Singing is singing, but helping people, that's a whole other way of living."

Leland slipped out of his jacket and handed it to Devon. He stood there and watched her sway down the hallway to the nearest bedroom. Over dinner she was all talk about how she was raised, and what it was like hooking up with the Pearly Gates. Even eating scrambled eggs at four in the morning somewhere on the other side of Des Moines, Iowa, was a big part of the process. Leland held his own but couldn't rival Devon when it came to big-city razzle-dazzle, though he did delve into his brother

Thaddeus and his early days at the University of Nevada, and his ravenous appetite to learn more about business and numbers.

"When did Carly first go on the run?"

"About three days after she was born."

Devon laughed. "I've heard of starting early but never quite like that."

"She's always been a handful, even as a kid. She clashed with the nuns at St. Anne's and we had to put her in public schools. From there it was spinouts and free-falls, but she always did her work, nearly straight A's all the way through."

"What a marvel she's been. They don't all lock in like she's done."

"Do you think she's had enough romping and stomping?"

"Now, we're not going there, especially right now. Not after the big spinout we've thrown her way."

"She'll survive, she's tough. All she needs to do is rest up."

Devon gave Leland a look, the same one she gave him that day in the lobby of the hotel. "Speaking of rest, why don't we go get some."

Leland walked her down the hallway to what he hoped was an evening of whispering in the dark and cooing in her ear. Beneath the sheets he told himself not to think about the size of her house and the wide expanse of her backyard and how many people on the other side of the fence were sitting around the dining room table eating roast beef with mashed potatoes. Instead he tried nuzzling and kissing but she twisted and turned in all the wrong ways. He pulled her even closer and said he wanted her more and more but his words felt dry and out of place. Somehow the warmth and loveliness of his tiny room was missing. Even Devon's sputtering moans and groans seemed out of rhythm with what they were trying to do.

"Come on baby, just relax now, we've got all night," Devon said.

Leland released a long column of breath and inhaled the scent of her perfume in the hope of igniting the switch that seemed so reluctant to turn over. In return Devon was soft and inviting. She tongued deep inside his mouth but came up empty. United, the divide only grew wider.

"I'm really missing the hotel," she said.

§

So the hotel became home to their erotic explorations. Night after night they cuddled and kissed and didn't give a damn who huddled in the hallway. And of course folks heard what they wanted to hear, and with that came gossip that spread through the place one layer at a time. But not one of the lonely hearts was brave enough to say anything to either one of them. After all, he was the ruler of the land.

As for Devon, she greeted everyone with a friendly wave and let it go at that. On some nights she even took to sitting in the lobby and watching TV with her newfound friends. They'd listen to the latest news emerging out of Vietnam and barely say a thing. Rice paddies and assorted body parts did little to awaken their tired souls. But it wasn't all heartache and despair. Often *Beat the Clock* would light them up with laughter, including Devon. They'd hone in on whatever stupid stunt the contestants were competing in, like tossing cups into a swinging bucket or popping a balloon with a tack. And when the cash prize would wing upward in the range of one to two hundred dollars, the downtrodden bunch would hoot and holler and Devon would be right there with them.

But she didn't stop there. She finally had a break-through with Carly and brought her into the fold. The two of them must have had three or four sit-downs before Devon broke through the hardness that Carly had been living in. One cold wintry night, Leland joined them and the three hungry hearts gathered in Devon's office. She and Carly talked about taking care of one's self, and Leland sat there doing his stoic best to listen to the newfound gospel that was seeping into their lives. The best moment came when they hugged it out on the front steps, first with Devon and Carly, then with Carly and her father. She pinned her chest to his and maybe for the very first time ever, he held her close to him.

Letting go, he stared at the plaque barely visible through the flying snow, the Holy Order of Recovered Sisters. Without them he knew that he and Dorothy could easily be pacing the floor at the hospital wondering if the tortured nights were ever going to end.

Nearly two weeks after that eventful night, Carly and Leland were standing behind the counter at the hotel.

"I guess I'm getting used to seeing Devon coming and going."

"Seems to like it here, best I can tell."

"Is she going to move in here permanently?"

"Does life get to be that good? She was joking the other day that she now owns a two-bedroom closet in northwest Reno."

"You know, you could move her into the room right next to yours and you could share the bath. That way you wouldn't have to go out in the hallway."

"We'll see, it's a little early for that."

"Just a thought."

"What's your mother think about all of this?"

"She doesn't say much. Harlan, on the other hand, well, he's had some things to say."

"Like what?"

"The usual, people should marry their own kind."

"Did he learn that at St. Anne's?"

"Couldn't tell you. I haven't been there in a while."

"So here we are, you, me, and Devon. Who'd a thunk?"

"It was never a black-white thing but more about recovery. I was afraid I wasn't going to make it."

"Keep listening to Devon, that's all I know."

§

Winter came with one blast after another. Record-setting snows lit up the town and froze it into place, but Leland soldiered on, stripping his drunks of whatever money they had and running it to the bank.

One night he and Devon chowed down at the Sky Tavern Buffet at the ShowCase Casino, basking in a wide array of tacos and pizzas with shrimp on the side. An evenly sliced piece of cheesecake finished off the evening, with Devon giggling between bites and offering Leland her very last tidbit on the end of her spoon.

On the way back to the hotel, they walked along hand-in-hand. There was some light hanging in the air and nearing the hotel, Devon said, "Let's save some steps and go through the alley."

Leland complied, why wouldn't he, it was the same alley he looked out on every night of his life.

"Are you seeing what I'm seeing?" Devon said.

Up ahead, not far from the hotel, Mrs. Dauer was rummaging through a can of rubbish.

"What do you think she's doing?"

"No telling with her," Leland said.

Devon poked him in the ribs and said, "Be nice, if nothing else."

Several steps later, they got a better look. Mrs. Dauer was stuffing a piece of Styrofoam into her oversized coat and filling up her pockets with little samplings of mustard and mayonnaise.

"Do you believe that?" Devon said.

"Maybe she's going around the bend."

"Maybe she's fucking hungry, did you ever think of that?"

"She lives on a pension, that's all I know."

"Apparently it's not enough."

"Maybe this is why she didn't want me storm-trooping her room. Maybe she had food tucked in all the corners."

Devon tugged on Leland's sleeve. "Let's turn around, we don't want to embarrass her."

In the room, Devon shed her heavy white parka and brushed a few flecks of snow out of her hair. "That's enough to make me sick."

"I tried helping her but I got nowhere."

"So, what did you do for her?"

"I tried cleaning up her room and I gave her a few tomatoes."

"A tomato isn't going to save her ass."

Leland leaned back in his chair and stared at his pretty girlfriend. This was the first flash of disdain he'd seen flash across her face since the big flare-up with Carly.

"The goddamn trash, do you believe that?" said Devon.

Soon after they took to bed but there was no hugging or kissing, not even a midnight romp. Devon clung to her side of the bed and Leland did much the same.

§

The next day the horror of seeing Mrs. Dauer digging through the trash didn't pass. Devon crawled out of bed and before she splashed water on her face, she started in on Leland again. "I have to say, I'm seeing this place in a different kind of way. Maybe I've been floating along on a pink cloud."

"It's my fault she's rattling around in the garbage cans?"

"No one is saying it's your fault."

"Could have fooled me."

"I'm saying it ain't right, you and me cozying it up while she's in there starving."

"Why do you think I started a garden? So I could help some people find their way."

Devon let go with a deep sigh. "But a couple of tomatoes ain't gonna cut it."

"Hauling dirt up and down the back steps wasn't exactly easy."

"It was great, but it was ritual. We need to step up our game."

"What the hell does that mean?"

"I don't know what it means, but eating out of the trash simply ain't right."

"No one is applauding it."

"I wonder how many others are doing it?"

"It's not like this is Overachievers Anonymous."

"This is no time to be cute."

Leland closed his eyes and thought of counting to ten. "Do you even know what I've been through? Drunks aren't the only ones who suffer."

"Seeing Dorothy hit the bricks couldn't have been easy."

"There's a little more to it than that. Shortly after she

left, my body was inhabited by a hum."

"Say that again."

"My body hummed night and day for nearly two years."

"I'm way lost here. Why don't you have a seat," Devon said, patting the bed next to her.

"Right after Dorothy moved out of the house, my body started humming and wouldn't stop."

"That's a little out-there for me."

"All I had to do was close my eyes and I could hear it. All day, every day, without ever having a day off."

"That's deep."

"Painful, is more like it."

"Do you still feel it?"

"Nope, it went away. I was up on the roof and I felt the hum surging through my body and it zipped up and out of me and I saw this giant bird up in the air. She was beautiful. I'm pretty sure her name was Aspasia."

Devon stared at Leland with one eyebrow arched higher than the other. "Trust me, I've heard a lot of stories but nothing like this."

"That's what got me thinking about cleaning up the place and planting a garden, even moving in here was a big part of it."

"You're like a shark, you have to keep moving or die."

"Something like that."

"Pyramid Lake was pretty much the same for me. I swear I could hear it talking to me."

"Just keep pushing, that's what I tell myself."

"But there's got to be more to it than tomatoes."

§

That evening Leland slept alone, Devon telling him she needed to think about this new ripple in the road for her. Later he found out she had wandered through her house pondering a bird named Aspasia and if she knew the man she'd been sleeping with nearly every night of the week for several months now.

It took some doing, but the two heated up again after some rigmarole on the phone. Back in the room, they nuzzled and purred, but they didn't take it up into the clouds. Devon ended many an evening by closing her eyes and drifting off into slumber. Leland would follow soon after, rolling into the middle of the bed and lightly pulling Devon closer to him.

Late one night Devon woke with a gentle stir like someone had tapped her on the shoulder. She sat up and pinned her back to the wall and gazed about the room. Breathing deeply, she nudged Leland in the side.

"Are you all okay?" he asked.

"What's below us?"

"What did you say?"

"Below us, what's down there?"

"Some would say hell."

"Not that below. Here in the hotel, what's underneath this room?"

"The storeroom, that's where I put my tools. I've even got some sandbags stacked up in there."

"How big is it?"

"Oh, it's good size. Maybe not as big as the lobby but fairly close."

"Bingo, that's it."

"That's it, what are you talking about?"

"What do you think of building a kitchen, maybe even a restaurant?"

Leland shot right up. "Have you gone mad?"

"I don't mean a restaurant, restaurant. Not for the

public, but for the folks here. For Mrs. Dauer and company."

Leland fell back into bed. All the fuss with Carly and the Holy Order had taught him to slow down and listen. "Tell me more."

"Why not a restaurant for the masses?"

"You plan to feed the masses right here at the Eleanor?"

"I don't mean the masses, the masses. I mean the masses living right here under this roof."

"All of them?"

"Not the tourists, we'll let them eat in the clubs."

"What are we going to cook, and how much are we going to charge for it?"

"That's it, nothing. We're gonna give it away for free."

"And how are we going to pay for it?"

"We'll pay for it with our money, you and me, we'll make it work."

"You want us to spend our savings on feeding these people?"

"Beats suffering, doesn't it? Besides, I'm not living here knowing that folks are slurping up food out of garbage cans."

"I guess that's what I've been trying to do ever since Aspasia, but I keep coming up short."

"No more symbolism. We gonna take it to the streets."

§

Later that day, the three of them hunkered down in the backroom, and Devon went over to Carly and let her know that feeding folks for free would send a note of liberation flying through the air that would make the Eleanor known up and down the avenues.

"Look at all this room, this is something else. If we could put some elbow grease into this, we could really get it on," Devon said.

Leland scrunched up his face and tried seeing his old storeroom in a new way. "Might be worth a try," he said.

No doubt they had the room. The place was cavernous with high-beamed ceilings and huge windows that looked out on to the alley.

"We could put the kitchen over there, complete with a serving area, and then we get some tables and put them right over there for people to sit on, and then we don't have to worry about them eating out of trash cans."

Carly, being fresh out of recovery, was still swimming in skepticism. "Isn't this going to cost a lot of money?"

"Certainly something to think about," Leland said.

Devon wouldn't let up. "Let's run the numbers and see what we come up with. Besides, I'm not asking you guys to dig deep and pay the entire bill. I've got some money in the bank."

"What about the cooking? Who's up for that?" Carly asked.

"I might be able to do it. I'll have to keep my eye on the garden, but I should be able to do both."

"Now, that's what I want to hear," Devon said.

Carly paced back and forth. "I know, let's get Harlan to build it for free. It's about time he conjured up his Catholic faith and put it into action."

"Let's put a hold on this right now. I don't want some Benedict Arnold roaming around the Eleanor," Leland said.

"Even if it means saving a lot of money?" Carly asked.

"But what about me?" Leland asked.

"The past is the past. Hopefully we've all learned that

by now," Devon said, shrugging.

"But my past about did me in."

"I might have to start schooling you just like I do the girls over at the Holy Order of Let's Get It On."

Carly slipped in between Devon and Leland and held court. "No harm in asking."

"I wouldn't mind meeting the man," Devon said.

"He's short," Leland said.

"So am I," Devon said.

"It's not the same thing."

§

A week later, the five notables met, Carly, Leland, Devon, Dorothy, and most of all, the big-time culprit Harlan O'Brady. If one didn't know better, they might have thought the heads of the five families were sitting down to discuss the latest Mafia killing.

Harlan was the first to speak up. "What's your vision here, a full-scale operation with three meals a day?"

"Heavens no, we're not up for something like that. We're thinking every evening we'd serve a single dish, like stew or lasagna. My family has all kinds of recipes. When it comes to cooking, black folks know how to do it up right," Devon said.

Harlan stared at Devon like he didn't know what to think. And Leland wondered if the man had any depth to him, let alone width. "If we have to do this on the cheap, so be it. The idea is to feed some folks who otherwise can't figure out how to do it themselves."

"I think it's a wonderful idea. I never have understood how some of these people get by," Dorothy said.

Devon slid across the floor to where Dorothy was standing. "You know this whole thing got started because we saw Mrs. Dauer eating out of the trash."

"That poor woman. I can't imagine how she lives."

Leland stood there and listened while the two women carried on, one his former wife and the other a lustful lover of a type of love he hadn't known anything about until Devon came along. "I guess we need to start with the kitchen. We'll have to round up a stove and make sure the building can be vented properly."

"Have to say, it looks doable. You'll need some room to prepare food and maybe a counter of some type," Harlan said.

"So it's a go?" Carly asked.

"Now, I didn't say that. Dorothy and I need to sit down and go over a few things. I've got a crew of workers to think about."

"We're not going to ask them to work for free, we'll have to figure something out, but there's nothing to worry about," Dorothy said.

§

Word came down through the airwaves, first to Carly and later on to Leland that Harlan had decided to reel himself up into the illustrious world of caring about someone other than himself. Leland heard the news and thought about the day at St. Anne's, the beginning of his new beginning. Working alongside Harlan might put a rub into his skin, but he needed to give it a go if he wanted to keep riding along with Devon at his side. She, on the other hand, skipped across the floor and performed an array of tiny dances, complete with a few whoops and hollers.

On the first go-around, Leland hauled sandbags up and down the back steps and slid them under a giant tarp in the basement. In the afternoons he set about hammering warped boards into place, which meant every other one, but by the end of the day he was halfway through and he told himself he'd put in a good day's work.

On day three it was him and Harlan working side-by-side like a couple of gunslingers, and they did so without a lot of words flowing back and forth. Harlan strolled through the door at precisely 7:00 a.m. sans any workers, only him and his overflowing bag of tools. The only jabbering that went on between the two was him telling Leland that his employees wouldn't be saddling up for a job that wouldn't do much when it came to keeping a roof over their heads. He said that he and Dorothy decided it was best if they kept the money flowing in and that way they wouldn't have to dip too deeply into their own reserves. That was the only way he could help with such a far-flung idea of feeding people for free.

The very idea that Dorothy and Harlan had been fussing over money made Leland's jaw tighten until it ached. From there a heavy dose of silence descended over both of them and nary a word tarnished the air for the rest of the day. Leland hid on one side of the room and pounded away on the floor, while Harlan busied himself with a measuring tape and a pad of yellow paper.

That evening, Leland holed up in his room with a large-sized pizza and devoured it with Devon's help. Between bites she wanted to know how everything about Harlan, otherwise known as the man willing to work for free.

"I didn't talk to the son-of-a-bitch."

"Not one little itty-bitty word?"

"Not many, that's for sure."

Devon scratched her head. "So that's how it's going to be?"

"What am I supposed to say? Thank you for ruining my life?"

"Is that how you feel, that your life is in ruins?"

Leland swallowed the last of his pizza. "I'm not saying that. Life has been good to me."

Devon drew a heavy breath and stared directly into his face. "Let's say that Harlan had never come along and that you'd be going along without any changes whatsoever."

Leland thought about what he'd been through, the hum and its irritating presence. From there it was onto Aspasia and a sense of liberation, all of it capped off by sliding under the covers with Devon nearly every night. "Now that you put it that way, that old life seems dead to me. Some of it I can't even remember."

"Now compare that to Harlan. Where is he in the mix, big or small?"

"I guess he's an insect of some kind."

"Now, do we go around squishing bugs or do we let them go?"

"Don't tempt me."

§

"How's it going back there?" Carly asked.

Leland gave the question some thought but not much.

"Make love, not war, I guess."

"That sounds like Devon talking."

"You got that right."

"Harlan's nice enough to do this for free, you have to give him that much."

"Doesn't mean I don't feel like popping him in the mouth."

Carly laughed. "You and me both, but he's not a bad guy, a little stiff around the edges."

"Is your mother happy?"

"They listen to a lot of music, I think that's a big part of it. Lately Dean Martin is playing every time I stop by for a visit."

"Just what the world needs, more Dean Martin."

From there it was another day of the Leland and Harlan extravaganza. Upon his arrival, Harlan announced a delivery of sheetrock was in the mix, it was just a matter of when.

"How much did that run you?"

"Two hundred and thirty-five dollars."

"I'll see you get reimbursed by the end of the day."

Harlan let loose with words about as readily as Leland, which meant one, then the other. "It's ours."

Leland turned and walked away. He and Dorothy had had their way with money, most of them hammered out in low groans and dark grimaces about there never being enough to go around.

At noon neither man had much choice but to turn and face the other. Leland grabbed a bag he had hiding under his coat, while Harlan slipped outside and snatched one off the dashboard of this truck.

"It sure is nice to see Carly looking so fresh," he said on his return.

"Who would have thought a place like the Holy Order could make so much headway in such a short amount of time?"

"Dorothy says people are ready when they're ready."

"Carly was overdue, to say the least," Leland said.

"She likes Devon a lot. She can't stop talking about her."

"Hence the name recovered sisters."

"I guess she has a lot of experience in these matters? Dorothy was telling me she used to drink a lot herself."

"She's a special person. She's here to help, that's for sure. This restaurant was her idea."

"You'd think she'd have her hands full over at her place."

"Between the three of us, we'll get it done. Besides, Devon spends a lot of time here anyway."

A long pause hit the airways.

"I hear she's up and moved in with you."

"She still has her own place."

Harlan's smile was brief and to the point. "You make for a different type of couple."

"We get all kinds of eyeballs on us. Here, the clubs, even the grocery store. Everyone needs a second look."

"We don't see many mixed couples in Reno."

"Let 'em stare, that's what I say."

§

Harlan maintained a steady hum to the way he worked. He'd show up after tending to business on his other jobs, and Leland spent his time hauling wood and hammering a nail or two. To his chagrin, he had to admit that Harlan knew what he was doing. Drilling holes and drawing lines on the floor didn't seem to throw him one bit.

"Do you think you're on schedule back there?" Carly asked one morning.

"We're making progress."

"Looks to me like we're headed for an opening sometime in early September."

The days of summer were coming to a close, and a touch of fall was seeping into his lungs most mornings. In between agonizing moments with Harlan, Leland could be found on his roof tending to his latest crop of juicy tomatoes. With some luck, he'd have them ready for opening night in the café. That way everyone would know that he was a real farmer, born and bred in the dirt and that his time upstairs wasn't silly or a waste of time.

And when he wasn't busy smelling the vines, he was staring at the rental board and counting the vacancies. Come winter, he knew his hotel would be as empty as some people's minds if it weren't for his band of minstrels.

"Maybe it will pick up by the weekend," Carly said.

Leland knew that was unlikely. One or two strong ones might make it over the pass and wander into the Eleanor, where they'd commence slinking up and down the street and feeding their hard-earned money into those metal contraptions that always took more than they ever gave back.

"There must be something we can do," Carly said.

"Wait it out, that's all I've ever done."

"I know what we can do. What about talking to the personnel office at the El Matador? They might be able to send people our way."

"Are you sure they'd be willing to help you?"

"I didn't tell them all to fuck off, just Phillips."

"Maybe you could rustle up some fry cooks."

§

After weeks of showing up, the place was finally taking shape. The floor had been smoothed into place, though Leland planned to sand and polish it after he painted the walls a soothing shade of white. Harlan had vented the wall and ceiling and built a counter, so Leland and company could hand out scrumptious meals to those in need.

Today's task was sheet-rocking and getting ready to paint. With luck Harlan thought that three days of highly focused work would bring the restaurant into view. Not finished or even close but at least it would start looking like a well-thought-out eatery. The trouble was he and Leland would have to work side-by-side with Harlan being the man in charge.

"Now we have to take one sheet at a time. I want you to hold it tight and I'll hammer it in place," Harlan said.

"I hear you," was the best Leland had to offer.

Over in the corner, Harlan had constructed large-sized scaffolding that both men had to climb onto, which they did with ease.

"Now, there's no need to rush through this, we want everything to look professional."

Leland nodded like a little boy on the school grounds, which didn't exactly make for a fun day, but sometimes being told what to do was a part of life and a part Leland had never warmed to.

He hoisted the first of many panels off the ground and with Harlan's help placed it high up on the wall.

"Put a strong grip on it and I'll do the rest," Harlan said.

Leland had to admire Harlan's work. He'd pluck a nail out of his pouch and hammer it into the wall, not once ever missing or having to take time to straighten the head and start all over again.

"How's that look?" Harlan asked.

Leland had no choice but to smile, though it was hardly the best he'd ever come up with. "Looks good, looks mighty good."

"Now if we do that about eight hundred more times, we'll be sitting pretty."

"Devon will be happy."

"So she's off saving souls today?"

"That's right. She's up and out the door pretty early most days."

"Do you think she'd ever consider bringing some of her girls over to St. Anne's? It might do them a world of good."

Leland paused and counted to three. St. Anne's was not high on his list of things to do. "She might consider it, though they like to keep the girls close to home through the early days of recovery."

"How long was she a heavy drinker?"

"Let's say she gave it a good, hard run."

"Seems like a lot of minority types have their struggles with alcohol."

"Couldn't tell you. Personally I give myself a beer every now and then but that's about it."

Sheet after sheet went up on the walls, first one, then another. Around noon, Leland heard the door open and he spotted Dorothy walking in the door with a large bag in her hand.

"I thought you gentleman might like something a little different, so I bought some tacos."

"That's awfully sweet of you," Harlan said, grabbing the bag and setting it on the counter. Rummaging through it, he came up with a taco about the size of a baseball and handed it to Leland. "Here, try one. They're just down the street. We eat there all the time."

Leland had to admit it was tasty. He took three large bites and nearly devoured the whole thing.

"This is coming right along, isn't it?" Dorothy said.

"Not without some doing," Leland said. "It's a marvelous idea. Why not help these people. After all, they supported us for many years."

Leland had to admit, it was pennies into dollars much of the way. Without his lost souls, his hotel would have vanished.

After four tacos apiece, Harlan wiped his hands and tossed the bag into the trash. "I was telling Leland that

Devon might consider bringing her girls over to St. Anne's. A little Catholicism never hurt anyone."

"It certainly never worked for Carly. I don't know how many times I tried getting her to join me," she said, shaking her head.

Leland couldn't help but render a mild protest. "She's doing all right. Just look at her. The front desk has never been so organized, and she's even got an idea on how to drum up some new business, and a lot of the credit needs to go to the Holy Order."

For a second Leland thought he saw chagrin spread across their faces, but Dorothy spoke up before his anger could mount.

"Maybe as a favor to us, you could mention it to her," Dorothy said.

Leland said sure, why not, though he wasn't sure he'd remember.

"Well, I have to run, I've got a young lady coming in this afternoon," Dorothy said.

"Thanks for thinking of us," Harlan said.

With that he leaned down and gave her a big round smack on the lips. And not only that, he did it until Leland could tell they were both getting aroused, and he had no choice but to stand there and stare at the drippy mess. A part of him wanted to succumb to his old way of being and reclaim what he believed to be his long-standing marriage to Dorothy. But he knew causing a scene was pro-bably the worst thing he could do, so he said, "I'll be right back," and he took off for O'Dells Fine Foods and Even Better Groceries and tried shaking himself free of what he'd just witnessed.

Inside the store, only one thing caught his eye, at least on his initial pass through, and that was Black Jack gum, named after the infamous Antonio Lopez de Santa Anna, a notorious and utterly ruthless killer who slayed many in the Texas War of Independence. Needless to say, given the measure of his despair, Leland couldn't help but understand the depth of the man's desperation.

While waiting in line, he gave the place a once-over. His eyes landed on a display not far from the front window. Sitting on top of one another was a large pile of marshmallows that came in a variety of reds, yellows, and blues. Pasted across each bag was the name Puffy and inside were tasty little balls of sugary goo. Just like that, Leland's mind shifted into overdrive and wouldn't let up. Why not give Antonio Lopez de Santa Anna something to smile down on from heaven, provided that's where he ended up.

Outside he quickly slipped a stick of gum into his mouth, and the anise flavor went a long way in soothing his brewing anger about seeing Dorothy and Harlan cuddling like desperate teenagers in the backseat of a car. But it also gave way to his vindictive side, which was bubbling up with newfound freedom.

So with his mind wild and ready for something new, he walked back to the hotel in one long soulful glide. Consequences be damned, he thought. Why couldn't he have some fun and act any old way he wanted?

Fortunately, he turned into the alley and saw that Dorothy's car was no longer there, which was for the better. After all, there was a chance that her Catholic way of being might weaken his resolve and the two dollars and eighty-seven cents he spent on marshmallows would go to waste.

Looking around, much like a thief in the night, he ripped open his bag and set about giving Harlan what he had coming. And despite the fact that Harlan was only on the other side of a wall, Leland unscrewed his gas cap and stuffed six sugar-ridden marshmallows into Harlan's gas tank, hoping they would gum up the works. And to make sure they did, he grabbed a stick from the other side of the alley and shoved the gooey mess into what had to be a fresh pool of gasoline most likely about four inches deep.

Crossing the alley, he stared down into a trashcan at a mass of broken bottles and torn-up pieces of newspaper. He immediately spit out his gum but yearned for a taste of the marshmallows that he hoped would pave his way to putting one over on Harlan and his maniacal way of kissing Dorothy right in front of him. With confidence he tipped his head back and plopped three marshmallows into his mouth and commenced sucking on what he thought was going to be the biggest thrill of his life.

Inside, he stared Harlan down and said, "Do you think we've got another section or two in us before we call it a day?" Leland asked.

Harlan nodded and said, "What's that sweet stuff I smell?"

Leland's eyes widened and his mind went back to work. "I bought some Sugar Babies up the street. They tasted so good I gobbled the entire bag. I didn't even think to get one for you."

"That's all right, I don't eat many sweets. I don't think they're good for you."

"That's what I hear."

After that quick exchange, the two of them took to lifting and hammering the sheetrock to where it needed to go. Each time Leland grabbed ahold of a panel, he took pride in knowing that he had put one over on Harlan, even if he had done it behind his back.

Close to five, Harlan slammed the last nail of the day into the wall with a thunderous whomp. "A few more days like this and you'll be ready to paint."

"I've painted plenty of walls in my day."

"I'll be sure and leave the scaffolding here until you're finished."

"Appreciate that."

Harlan grabbed his coat and headed for the door. "See you first thing in the morning."

"I'll be here."

Leland hung back but made sure he had a full view of Harlan's van through the front window. He watched him climb inside and fumble with his key. And then he hit it with a hard twist and the engine moaned but that's all it did. Starting was out of the question. He tried it several more times but nothing happened. He let loose with a few cuss words that ran afoul of his Catholic training, but luckily for him, the only one to hear them was Leland, and he was too busy swimming in full support of what he'd done.

Walking outside, Leland tapped on the side window.

"I see you got a problem?"

"Damn thing won't start. Sounds like the battery, but I just replaced it a few months ago."

"Could be a short in the wiring."

"More like it's time for a new van. I've had nothing but trouble over the last year."

Poor you, Leland thought. Let me tell you what a rough year is really like. "I can give you a ride home if need be."

"I'll call Dorothy. We'll grab a bite to eat, then try it again. Maybe I flooded it. If that doesn't work, I'll probably have to have it towed."

"That's a shame."

"Life is full of surprises."

"Sure is, especially the ones you never see coming."

§

Leland was in his chair sipping the last of his morning coffee. Devon was in the far corner slipping into a silky pair of slacks and a brightly colored vest. Much of the time she was mumbling about living in New York which was way beyond Leland's range of knowing. Glancing at his watch, he knew Harlan would be outside fairly soon, climbing out of Dorothy's car. Hopefully his van was out in the desert, exactly where it needed to be, dying a lonely death due to an overdose of sugar.

"Now, you have a nice day," Devon said, leaning down and kissing Leland on the cheek. "In a few more weeks we'll be serving food like we're master chefs."

Leland leaned back and soaked up the pleasure of knowing that Devon was happy. But before he could say anything, there was a knock on the door.

"Little early for company, wouldn't you say?" Devon said.

"I'm not in the mood for any."

Devon opened the door and standing two feet away from her was Carly with her hands on her hips and her face streaked in blotches of red.

"What's wrong, did something happen downstairs?" Devon asked.

"Ask him," she said, pointing at her father.

"Did I make a mistake with the deposit?"

"I wish."

"Carly, we have no idea what you're talking about," Devon said.

"He knows damn well what I'm talking about. He

damaged Harlan's gas tank with a bunch of marshmallows."

"You what?" Devon said, spinning and staring directly into Leland's face.

He sat straight up like he'd been jammed in the back. "I did no such thing."

"Who else, then?"

"You know damn well all kinds of people wander up and down the alley."

"Harlan even found the bag of marshmallows in the trash. It's a wonder he didn't have it dusted for prints."

"He won't find mine on them."

"He said you came back from lunch smelling of sweets."

"Those were Sugar Babies."

"When did you start eating that crap?" Devon asked.

"My sweet tooth had me going crazy yesterday afternoon."

"Well, Harlan believes you did something and Mom spent the evening weeping in the corner. I guess you can kiss your café goodbye."

"We can survive without him. He isn't the only one who knows what to do with a hammer."

Devon fell backward onto the bed. "But he's been so nice with everything."

"We'll get along just fine without him. Let him go back to St. Anne's and pray. Maybe they'll talk to him about Judas one of these days."

"Then you admit it. You did vandalize his van," Devon said.

"I did not damage that man's van, and I don't need to hear a damn thing about it."

"Well, he thinks you did," Carly said.

"Who knows how that man thinks."

Devon leaned into Leland's face and let go with her most sincere thoughts on the matter. "You best not be lying to me, Leland. That isn't how I've come to terms with how I live my life."

"Who gives a fuck about marshmallows."

§

Devon and Carly blustered out the door, and Leland made sure he held his firm manner until the sound of their shoes faded in the hallway, then he slumped into his chair and stared at the wall for a good forty minutes.

Later he dove into a less-than-friendly meal up the street. Given his mood, he liked lathering into the grease that only a fat piece of meat had to offer. It helped his mind and his newfound quarrel with telling the truth. Up to now it had always been his friend, a credo born out of the land and honed into him by his demanding father. He told him one day that a lie was a betrayal of a man's soul, but Leland had to admit that taking Harlan for a ride was like sitting around the house in your underwear watching *Perry Mason* while slurping down a bowl of ice cream smothered in heavy syrup and that was about as good as it gets.

Of course Carly was right, come nine o'clock there was no sign of Harlan strolling through the door with a hammer in one hand and a box of nails in the other. He was just glad that Dorothy wasn't there to take him down a notch with a volley of words he didn't need to hear.

He spent much of the day sweeping out the backroom and sorting out his next move. Finishing without someone's help was nearly impossible, and there wasn't anyone around the hotel who was strong enough to make a difference.

That evening he slumped in his chair with a roast beef

sandwich and was halfway through it before Devon opened the door and gave him a questioning smile.

"How was work?" he asked.

"Reasonable, I guess. We had a new girl come into the program. There's a good chance she's going to give us a run for our money. And you?"

"Got a few things done. Not much though. Had to do everything by myself."

"So no Harlan?"

"Not a hair. After all, Dorothy could have dropped him off if he wanted to help us."

"Not if he's mad."

"No reason to be mad at me."

"Leland, are you sure about this?"

Before Leland could rattle off an answer, there was a knock on the door.

Devon opened the door and found one very angry Carly staring at them. "Carly, are you all right?"

"Harlan and his mechanic sawed his gas tank in half and sure enough they found three marshmallows floating inside."

"Well, they weren't mine."

"Oh, is that right? For your information, I walked over to O'Dells just now and asked them if they remembered selling you a bag of marshmallows."

"They sure the hell don't remember every transaction."

"He remembered yours. Not many people buy Black Jack gum and a bag of marshmallows."

"That's impossible."

"I thought you bought Sugar Babies?" Devon asked.

"I did."

"A pack of Black Jack gum fell out of your jacket last

night."

"I bought both."

"Who buys gum and Sugar Babies?"

"He said he remembered you because of the fiendish look in your eye," Carly said.

Leland stared down at the floor but didn't say anything.

"Leland, if you did something, now is the time to tell us," Devon said.

"I keep telling you, I'm an innocent man."

"My ass," Carly said.

"Why would the man at O'Dells lie to us?" Devon asked.

"Maybe he's some sort of goofball."

Carly shook her head. "Unbelievable, my father is a bold-faced liar."

"Leland, I've come too far to start living like this," Devon said.

"I think I need to be left alone."

"If you're lying to me, you're gonna be left alone for a long, long time."

"And you can kiss the restaurant goodbye," Carly said.

With that both women fled the room, first Carly, then Devon. Leland plopped into his chair and finished his sandwich. The taste was different now. A couple of bites, and he felt like spitting up on the floor.

§

The next morning Leland rolled over in bed. A restaurant was still to his liking, but without Devon and a touch of her bankroll, the idea of free food for his lost souls seemed frivolous.

For now coffee was his only answer. He sat in his chair and sipped until he could sip no more. A small part of him glistened at the thought of taking Harlan down a notch or two, but the idea of Devon disappearing into the night was enough to destroy his vision of life.

That thought alone lit a flame to his inner self, the same one that tried freeing the hotel of its raunchy smell and gave him the idea to plant a garden on his rooftop. He was now convinced that a brightly colored café would subdue Devon's anger and lure her back into their lovely little nest, otherwise known as the Eleanor Hotel.

Downstairs he saw there was no way to finish by himself. He knew he needed help. He hopped into his truck and flew down the road, past the clubs and through the heart of a so-so neighborhood. Near the river, he came upon the Nevada State Hospital, home to those with flinty minds and rambunctious ways. For some reason, unbeknownst to him, men looking for a few dollars' worth of work lined up in front of it and waited for those with money to descend upon them.

Leland was no fool when it came to desperation. He wasn't about to get bundled up and tossed into the river just because he had a few bills in his pocket. For that reason alone, he slowed his truck down and saw men of all shapes and sizes, not to mention the looks in their eyes.

The first fellow that came into view was a thunderous-looking man with bulging muscles and dangerous-looking forearms. Slowing down, he gave him a once-over and saw a tattoo that read, "I Love My Mother But . . ."

In a panic, he stepped on the gas and flew around the block, so he could gather himself once more. This time he thought only of men in groups of two and threes. Finally he spotted the ones he needed. A couple of broken-down slobs who couldn't rob him if they had an arsenal about the size of the National Guard.

"How are you guys getting along today?" Both men looked like it was more than they could comprehend. "It's a sheet-rocking job downtown and pays three dollars an hour."

Like the nomads they were, they stared at one another and were most likely transferring dollars into wine. Once they were finished with the math, the smaller of the two found the time to speak up.

"Lead the way, we're pretty sure we can handle this."

Leland nodded in the direction of the truck and motioned for them to climb in the back. Of course this took some doing seeing how neither was very agile, and they were treating the truck like it was Mt. Everest. The last thing Leland wanted was to grab either one of them by the butt and give them a good hearty push. After all, there was a limit to how far he'd go to give Devon her dreamy little café and all that went with it and a butt was one of them.

Turns out their names were Melvin Jones and Henry Lee, both from the South but hardly long-lost friends. Later they told Leland how they'd met up at a food line not far from the hotel and discovered they had a lot in common, which meant they liked to drink every day.

Back at the hotel, Leland's voice dropped a notch as he explained how the job was supposed to go. He wanted Melvin alongside of him and Henry Lee to help lift the sheets up off the ground.

At first the plan went well. It appeared both men had manual labor tucked deeply into their calloused-looking skin. With every panel, Melvin pressed them to the wall and let Leland let fly with his hammer.

Off the start, he was wild and coarse, and it wasn't until the third panel that he found his way. The more he pounded, the more he relived his ballsy adventure into Harlan's gas tank and the many ways it took him down a peg or two.

The trouble didn't start until they were about halfway across the room. Henry Lee turned and nudged Leland in the ribs. "I'm awfully dry, my friend."

"Sure buddy, there's a jug over there by the wall."

Henry Lee did find his way across the room, and he began slurping water until Leland thought he might drown. So he couldn't help giving him the same look he gave renters when they were telling him why their money had run out.

Luckily Henry Lee came up for air, but Leland made a mental note to drink from another bottle when he got thirsty.

Within seconds they were up and at it again, but it wasn't until a few minutes later that Henry Lee grabbed his back and let go with a giant scream. "I think I pulled something," he said, standing sideways and rubbing his back.

"You need to walk it off, we've still got a lot of work to do."

"Man, this ain't the Super Bowl. Let's see if he's all right," Melvin said.

Henry Lee leaned against the wall and for a second there, Leland thought he was going to tear up. "We might have to finish up tomorrow."

"Now, I know what you boys have in mind. You'll take what few dollars you have coming and I'll never see you again."

"Then you go back down to the river and get another couple of fly-by-nights to help you out," Henry Lee said.

"No, we're not doing that. My love life is hanging in

the balance, and I plan to be over at my lady friend's house this evening telling her we have the storeroom finished, and that I'll be ready to paint in the morning."

"You can't ask a man to work if he's all crippled up," Melvin said.

Leland put on the muscle like he rarely did and stared right into the eyes of Henry Lee. "I'm saying you have to push through the pain and that's all there is to do it."

"Now, no one wants trouble," Melvin said.

"Then let's get up on the scaffolding and knock out a few more."

"Maybe my back is calming down," Henry Lee said.

With that they were off and running. The two down-and-outers did all the lifting, and Leland followed through with the hammering. An hour later, he said, "We could knock off and get a bite to eat."

"We'd like to finish up and get out of here," Melvin said.

Henry Lee concurred with a big nod and three hours later Leland said with firm conviction, "One more sheet will do it."

"I'm not sure I've got one more in me," Henry Lee said.

"My arms are about to give out," Melvin said.

The two friends lifted the last piece in the air but Melvin had trouble holding it in place.

"Let me help," Henry Lee said, jumping up on the scaffolding and inching his way toward his friend.

"You need to scoot it up one more notch if you can," Leland said.

"We're trying," Henry Lee said.

The two weary men drew their breath and gave the sheet a heave-ho. Leland pressed his shoulder into it and hammered until his knees sagged and it looked like even his will was about to give out.

He gave the wall another couple of whacks and then took a couple of steps back. "Gentlemen, I think we've got it."

All three of them climbed off the scaffolding and stared up at the ceiling. The last piece was close to being properly aligned but it was off by about a quarter of an inch right where the two walls came together.

"We could pry it off and give it another go," Melvin said.

"Looks good to me, I think we can call it a day," Leland said.

The two rummies leaned against the wall while Leland went inside to get some money.

"Love does funny things to people," Henry Lee said.

§

That evening rain splashed against his window and filled the tiny gutters running through the alley. If it weren't for Devon, he could have easily laid in bed rubbing his sore hips and wondering if he had it in him to paint the café all by himself. Around eight he showered and shaved and looked outside. Still the water was flashing across the streets but waiting for it to stop would have sent him into a tizzy. If Devon got too used to being alone, she could be like a meteorite that had flashed through his life and disappeared. That alone caused a pain to shoot through his lower half and nearly tip him over.

Outside he got in his truck and headed down the road. A phone call would have been all right, but he needed a face-to-face, even if it were for the last time. Luckily her car was parked in the driveway and a single light was burning in the living room. She was probably reading about pain and suffering in the modern era.

He rang the bell with a light touch but no one opened the door. A part of him wanted to flee, another needed to regroup and settle in again. He pushed the button one more time and the light in the room flashed off and the one in her bedroom flicked on.

He rang the bell again but nothing happened. Oh boy, he thought, she must be mad. He might have to live with his marshmallow folly for a long, long time. Turning, he crossed the driveway and opened the door to his truck. By now the rains had picked up and his jacket was wet through and through. Damn it, it wasn't like he shot someone, he thought. Besides, he gave Harlan something to pray about while he sat yearning to connect with Saint Michael, the patron saint of all things just.

Behind the wheel, but with the engine running, he thought of his room back at the hotel. The thought of living there minus the bliss of Devon's company was more than he could bear. The very least she could do was say goodbye to his face.

He climbed back out and thought about tapping on her bedroom window but worried how it might look. Maybe someone would think he was a burglar and rain down a volley of bullets on him. He had no choice but to pick up a handful of pebbles and toss them at her bedroom window. At first nothing happened. Her light remained on and her curtain pulled closed.

Finally he saw the curtain peel back and the window open several inches. Her small round face and the soft glint of her eyes came into view. "Have you gone crazy?"

"I'm hoping we can sort this out."

"I think we need to think for a while."

"I know I did a goofy thing, I couldn't help myself."

"You got that right."

"But something came over me, it was like a curse."

"Destructive is what I call it. That man didn't deserve anything like that."

"Least let me come inside so we can talk about it," Leland said.

"Well, you're gonna drown if you stay out there."

Leland could have dropped to his knees and shouted hallelujah.

"Now don't let water drip all over my carpet," Devon said, opening the door.

Leland stepped inside and slipped out of his jacket. By now it was thoroughly drenched and most likely done for good.

"Come inside and I'll make you some tea. You know, a phone call would have been nice," Devon said, placing two cups on the table and filling them with water.

"Like I was saying, I couldn't help myself."

"But you lied to me and Carly."

"I know I did."

"And right to our faces and more than once, I might add."

"I was hoping to wiggle my way out of trouble."

"But that's not who I am. I don't slip and slide through life."

"And I've been known to do business on a handshake."

Leland sipped his tea and stared down at the table. Devon remained upright, still clinging to her moral high ground.

"I saw those marshmallows and went a little crazy."

"You dope, why'd you have to go and mess everything up?" Devon said, lightly slapping Leland across the head.

"What am I gonna do with my little farm boy?"

"We could roast some marshmallows if you like."

"This is no time to be cute."

Leland leaned forward and kissed her on the lips. "Let's put it behind us."

Devon hung in there longer than Leland would have guessed. "Let's go back to the hotel," he said.

"I sure do miss the place."

"It ain't the same there without you."

"There's something in the air there, I'm not sure how you've done it."

"Just wait until we get the café up and running."

"Know one thing, big fella, you're on probation with me."

"I hear what you're saying."

§

Back at the hotel, Devon fell into bed and stared up at the ceiling. Leland could tell right away that erotic delight would not be part of the discussion for quite some time.

"Are you still mad at me?" he asked.

"More like exhausted."

In the morning Leland woke to find one serious-looking Devon staring at him from across the room. "How'd you sleep?" he asked.

"My dreams had me coming and going."

"Pyramid Lake dreams?"

"Yep."

"So you saw the future?"

"More like I can see today."

"Meaning?"

"Carly and I aren't the morality police, and it ain't our job to drag you through the fires."

"That's nice to hear."

"But I saw the hotel on a giant set of stilts and it was leaning to one side."

"But it isn't on stilts."

"Are you sure about that?"

"Are you saying I made it this way?"

"I'm thinking you damaged its heart."

"And I'm thinking you think too much."

"I'm saying lying took this place in the wrong direction."

"All this with one fib?"

"If you want a special place, you have to act in a special way."

"But how would the hotel know I lied?"

"Something around you knows."

"That's a lot to ponder."

"I suggest you get to pondering."

"All because of some marshmallows?"

"This ain't no game we're playing here.

§

For the next few days, he thought he was in bed with a zombie from the other side of the world. At night she would dive under the covers and fall asleep, barely mumbling a word he could call their own. And sometime around two or three, she would let loose with a slew of mumbo-jumbo that Leland couldn't understand. His only hope was that she was on the verge of mending the way the hotel dreamed about itself.

After another week of going on and on about being in the desert, she nudged Leland in the ribs and said, "I think I've got it. It's about trust. The hotel needs to know you're on its side."

"The hotel is saying this to me?"

"Hey, baby, you're the one who started wiping the

place free of dust. Once you start that, there's no looking back. Bad smells won't stand for it."

"You dreamt all this last night?"

"I went deep, deep enough I think I'm on the right track. I saw a long stretch of farmland with tiny crystals flaring up and down as far as I could see."

"What the hell does that mean?"

"It means the truth will spin you free."

"And how is that going to happen?"

"We need to get some crystals and go to work around here."

"All of this because of some marshmallows?"

"I'm beginning to think sugar is one bad scene after another."

§

"Are you sure this is going to work?"

"It's worth a try. And besides, if it doesn't, I'm not sure I want to be living in a hotel as lopsided as this one."

"But I don't know anything about crystals."

"You don't have to, all you have to do is come along for the ride. The rest is up to me."

While Devon scurried off to the Lighter Than Light Crystal Shop, Leland set about slopping the walls with primer and smoothing it out with long even strokes that he knew oh so well. After all, he was no stranger to wire brushes and empty buckets of paint. Over the years he'd freshened every room in the hotel many times, and he'd been the sole owner of the cuss words that went along with it.

After three hours of smelling paint, Devon came strolling into the café carrying a brown paper bag. "That lady Clarissa was something else. We ended up having a therapy session."

"What you'd talk about?"

"Everything. You, me, Carly, the whole flare-up with Harlan and Dorothy."

"You tell her about my marshmallows?"

"Honey, I had to."

"What'd she say?"

"She said there's more than one way to be human, but you did take a step to the side, there's no denying that."

"And?"

"She said crystals might do the trick, it all depends."

"On what?"

"On how deep the wound is."

"Did you tell her about Aspasia?"

"Had to."

"Does she think I'm crazy?"

"Hardly, she thinks you blew the doors off and let the wind come in. But that's the problem, once you've gone that far, there's no turning back. We're in this for life."

"Oh boy."

"She said to give them a try, and if it doesn't work, she'll come over and take a look around."

"But how will we know if it's working?"

"Hopefully Pyramid Lake will let me know."

That evening they went to work, with Devon leading the way. "As soon as I got home, I slipped nine stones in a bowl of salty water. One is amethyst and the others are smoky quartz. That should rid them of any negativity they may have picked up along the way."

"Then what?"

"We're going to play farmer and plant them in the garden," Devon said, handing a big sack of stones to Leland.

Leland ran his thumb across the sharp edges of the

amethyst and marveled at the smoothness of the smoky quartz.

"This shouldn't take long, I've been homing in on the details ever since I saw a field of sparkling lights in my dreams."

Leland put his arm around Devon and pulled her tightly to his chest. "Why don't we relax before we go upstairs to the garden."

"No way, baby, we gotta make this right first, then we'll give some thought to snuggling like we used to."

Leland blew a long column of air out of his mouth and said all right.

"All we need is a hand trowel."

"There's one up in the garden."

They rode to the top of the elevator and into the coolness of the air and the bright glow of the moon. The vines were rich and full of fruit, though they were more green than red. The hope was that a little boost from the crystals would put them over the top.

"Who knows, the tomatoes might dig this," Devon said.

"This might make them redder than red can be."

A friendly smile flashed across Leland's face, the first one in a while.

"See, what we want to do is plant a grid in the middle of the garden and the rest is up to them," Devon said.

"Who should do this, you or me?"

"You're the farmer but I'm the one who had the dream, so maybe I should do it."

"But I'm the one who screwed up."

"I'm in the flow, best to leave me alone."

Devon went to work with Leland right beside her. She grabbed the trowel and plopped it alongside her right knee.

"We'll put the amethyst in the center and place the quartz around it in a pattern."

The stone was about four inches thick and smooth on one side and had sharp sparkling ridges on the other. Devon squished it into the soil and stared at it like she was in a room all by herself. "Now the trick is to place the quartz around it so each piece is spaced just right. I'm thinking about five inches will do it."

"Should I get a tape measure?"

"I don't think we want a lot of contraptions around here. I need to do this by feel."

Devon grabbed each smoky quartz and nuzzled them around the amethyst one by one. After she had four in place, she stopped and stared at them. "I think that's about right." She continued on at the same comfortable pace. When she finished, she stood up and gave herself a slight clap of the hands. "That should do it."

"Now what?"

"Now we cover them with some dirt and let them have their way."

Leland closed his eyes and came close to whispering a prayer. Trouble was, he didn't know any.

§

Leland walked into the back room knowing one thing. A crystal was a crystal and a garden was a garden but sweat and grime were what he knew best.

"What are we supposed to do now?" Carly asked.

"We put our heads down and see if we can't finish this off fairly soon."

"As long as it looks snazzy, that's more and more apparent to me. We don't want these people eating slop in some backroom dungeon, even if it is free. Above all else, we have to show them some class," Devon said.

"What about menus? Who's going to take care of that?" Carly asked.

"You two worry about that," Leland said.

"Chef Leland says he wants to do all the cooking," Devon said.

"I cooked many a day on the farm, lasagna, stew, things like that. One meal fits all."

"And tomatoes right from the rooftop," Devon said.

"You two work on that and picking out the paint. I'm about done priming and you need to figure out what you want to do with the floors."

"This is way too dusty. We can't have this around food," Devon said.

"And remind me to call the guy about the stove, it should have been here before now," Leland said.

"Let's relax, I think we're getting there," Devon said, wrapping her arm around Leland and giving him a light hug.

"What do you think, are the crystals lighting up our world like we hoped?"

"Too early to tell, but I know one thing, I've slept better the last few nights."

"Have you seen the shoreline lately?"

"Not since the crystal shop. I'm not too sure what to think."

Carly's forehead furrowed, and she walked away, not in a huff but lost somewhere inside her head.

"So how she's doing?" Leland asked.

"She's hanging in. She didn't exactly warm to the talk about crystals."

"You have to admit, it is a little out there."

"So are gas tanks full of marshmallows?"

"Hopefully she'll come around, but telling her about

Aspasia was probably one of the dumbest things I ever did. I can tell she doesn't get it."

"We play it straight down the middle at the Holy Order. We don't talk about crystals or visitations from Pyramid Lake, let alone big birds coming out of the sky."

"As long as she keeps the front desk running smoothly, we should be all right."

"She seems to be on top of it. I haven't heard anything about going back into the clubs."

"She's got a knack for numbers. Everything is signed off to the tee."

"Now we sit back and wait for the magic to rain down on us."

"I hope it doesn't rain too hard."

"It better rain some, let me tell you."

§

Devon was all about color schemes and little else. She and Carly took off to the paint store as if they were on a holy mission. Greens, browns, and lavenders were up for discussion. Over dinner she and Leland would study color samples and think about things like whether to use eggshell or semi-gloss. And of course, the very fiber of life depended on making the right choice.

Finally, over dinner at the ShowCase, Devon snapped open with a click of her fingers. "I've got it. Beige with white. Quiet but purposeful. It's important that everyone feels comfortable."

The next day Leland stepped up and took charge. "I think the linoleum squares with light green speckles running through them will do the job."

And Devon was right there with him. "We'll pick up a few boxes the next time I'm on that end of town."

"And the guy with the stove better wake up and

deliver. It's been over a week now."

"We might have to go talk to him," Devon said.

"We need to go tell him enough is enough."

"Now, we'll have none of that. Not after what we've been through. Besides, he's the only one in town who carries gas stoves. We need him more than he needs us."

Leland hemmed and hawed but didn't come up with anything.

"You know, this could be a sign," Devon said.

"A sign of what?"

"A sign the hotel is still going sideways."

"And maybe it means the guy messed up on the order."

"If only life were that simple."

And with that Devon delved back into her own brand of funk. For several days she slipped and slopped like Leland wasn't even in the room. At night it was more of the same. She wouldn't offer up a midnight kiss or say how are you doing in the morning. If Leland didn't know better, he would have thought she was getting ready to fall back into the sauce. Finally, after about a week, she spoke up and it wasn't with bits of gold flowing out of her mouth, but what she said made a smidgen of sense.

"We need to get Clarissa down here to take a look around. Something isn't quite right here."

"But what about the crystals? Did they or didn't they do their job?"

"Oh, they've been helpful, no doubt about that, but we're still flying sideways in the wind."

"But how can you tell?"

"Just a feeling. But that stove should have been here by now."

§

That evening Devon came back acting like she was thoroughly alive. Smiling at Leland, she let loose with why she thought everything was going to be all right. "I spoke with Clarissa and she's going to be here in the morning."

"And do what?"

"She's going to walk around and tell us what she sees."

"Is she some sort of witch?"

"Hell no, she ain't no witch. She's a lady who's been hanging out in a crystal shop soaking up the vibe."

"Let's hope."

"Hope is right, baby, because I have no interest in living on a sinking ship."

The next morning the phone rang and Devon answered right away. "That was Carly. She said Clarissa is in the lobby."

"What should I do?" Leland asked.

"Sit back, this will take less than a second."

Leland plopped in his chair and waited out the time. In less than five minutes, the door opened and in walked Clarissa.

"I want you to meet Leland Powers, the man I've been telling you about," Devon said.

Standing before him was a thin woman with blonde hair and sour-looking cheeks wearing black slacks and a loose-fitting green sweater. Somehow he was expecting blazing dark eyes and spikey blue hair.

"Nice to meet you. Devon has told me so much about you and the hotel. I have to say I'm quite impressed."

"Why is that? I haven't done much."

"But I have to differ. Devon told me how you came to live here and how you campaigned to rid the place of that musty odor."

"Have to say, I didn't do so well with that one."

"But now there's a garden and a café. This is all very special if you ask me."

"Did Devon tell you about the marshmallows?"

"She did."

"And?"

"We all have our moments, don't we? But on the other hand, revenge does take its toll."

Devon clapped her hands. "Let's not dwell in the negative. Why don't we take Clarissa on a tour."

The three of them bled into the hallway and with his first few steps, Leland surmised it was best if he didn't say much.

"Have to say, it feels quite homey in its way," Clarissa said.

"We have to hand it to Leland for that one," Devon said.

"But some aren't so comfortable, are they? There's a certain level of distress hiding behind these walls."

"Well, this is downtown Reno," Leland said.

"Being cast aside is never easy."

"I never did that in my life," Leland said.

Clarissa shook her head. "No, it's not you. It's what they've been through before they got here. It appears many are quite wounded."

"I told you she was good," Devon said.

Clarissa smiled and nearly laughed. "The smell certainly does get in the way. I see why you did what you did."

"How about we go upstairs?" Devon said.

The three of them slipped into the elevator and rode it up to the top.

"How many rooms here?"

"Forty-nine," Leland said.

"And how many people live here year-round?"

"Nearly half, the rest are tourists. They come and go."

Devon spoke right up. "I'm not too sure what to think of them. They don't strike me as being sincere."

"They have their minds on getting rich," Leland said.

"You mean the dream that never comes true?" Devon asked.

"Something like that."

Halfway down the hallway, Clarissa stopped. "Oh my, it's different in through here. Who is the person living in this room?"

"It's Mrs. Dauer, she's the one I told you about," Devon said.

Clarissa closed her eyes and breathed deeply. "Oh my, she's really festering. Has she been here a long time?"

"A good ten to twelve years. I can't say we've always gotten along either."

"Is she argumentative?"

"I wouldn't say that. She has very little to do with any of us. She pays her rent the first of every week and goes about her way."

"Out to the trash cans, that's where she goes," Devon said.

"We don't know if she does it all the time."

"Once is once too many," Devon said.

"She's been through a lot, that's for sure," Clarissa said, closing her eyes.

"I know very little about her," Leland said.

"I'm getting there was a father who wasn't very nice. Maybe a husband who was much the same."

"You can tell that?"

"Only a hunch, I could be way off."

"I doubt that," Devon said.

"I'm getting that there was wealth somewhere along the line. Maybe her father wasn't the most savory person you'd ever meet. Do you know where she's from?"

"I'd have to dig up her registration card, it's probably somewhere in the basement."

"I'm thinking Southern California. She did have sunlight in her life at some point."

Leland shrugged.

"What's important to know is that she's doing what so many of us do. We punish ourselves without ever knowing why. Does she gamble?"

"Penny slots, from what I hear."

"Figures, doesn't it? Some of us never know how to get rich."

"So now what?" Devon asked.

"It's very unlikely we're going to change her. She seems entrenched."

"So that's it, we're stuck?" Devon asked.

"I didn't say that. But the best we can do is smudge the air and see what happens."

"What does that mean?" Leland asked.

"I can burn some sage. It might help with several of them, but we'll probably have to do it periodically."

"So what do we do?" Leland asked.

"It's best if we do the entire hotel. That way we won't miss anything. I'm assuming there's a basement here."

"Of course."

"I take it it's pretty crowded."

"I'd have to say yes to that."

"You're cooking with gas, Clarissa," Devon said.

"And we should probably do it after midnight. That way everyone will be settled."

"But we can't go into their rooms. That would be

asking too much."

"Would be nice if we could get into her room."

"But she'll be asleep."

"We'll figure something out," Devon said.

§

"We need you to help us lure Mrs. Dauer out of her room for about fifteen to twenty minutes," Devon said.

Carly leaned back on the couch and stared at her father like maybe he'd finally taken a step too far. "You'd wake me up and have me come down here at 12:30 in the morning because of Mrs. Dauer?"

"If we want the café to be a success, then this is something we need to do."

Harry, the new man on graveyard, stared at them from across the lobby. Leland turned and nodded as if to say he wanted him to turn off his ears and go away.

"What exactly am I supposed to do?" Carly asked.

"A friend of ours will be here at any moment, and we're going to see if we can't liven up the hotel."

"But what's that got to do with Mrs. Dauer?"

"Let's just say we're going to smoke her out," Devon said.

"Come again?"

"We'll explain later, but for now we want you to tell her that there is a young boy down here claiming to be her grandson."

"How cruel is that?" Carly said.

"We know but we don't know how else do it," Devon said.

"Besides, she's a tough old bird, she'll survive," Leland said.

"Just remember, the café is going to take the Eleanor to new heights."

Carly shook her head and said, "I guess I'm here to serve."

"Our friend is supposed to meet us out back, and if you smell a little smoke, there's nothing to worry about," Devon said.

"It's been a while since I've told a bunch of lies."

"We all need to reminisce now and then," Leland said.

Devon fled to the back alley with Leland right behind. In less than a minute, a pair of headlights came into view and they knew Clarissa was headed their way.

"This place is gonna sing," Devon said.

"Right now it ain't nothing but what it is."

Clarissa pulled over to the side and rolled down her window. "Is the coast clear?"

"We sure hope so," Devon said.

"I don't want to startle an old woman in her sleep."

"Carly is going to have her sitting in the lobby, but we have to get going," Devon said.

"I have everything I need right here. We'll start in the basement and work our way up," Clarissa said, stepping out of her car holding a ball of sage in one hand and a tortoiseshell in the other.

The three of them slithered down the back end of the Eleanor and into the lobby. Carly was standing by the front desk and at the first sight of them jammed her thumb in the air with a firm conviction of a job well done.

"Okay, let's hurry," Devon said.

Downstairs Clarissa nodded and said, "Pretty much like I imagined. All these boxes and suitcases tell a story, don't they."

"Can't argue with that one," Leland said.

"What's next?" Devon asked.

"It's important we start with the door frames. There's

no telling what might have seeped in from the back alley," Clarissa said.

"And the luggage too. Look at all of this," Devon said.

Every nook and cranny were filled with duffel bags and suitcases that looked like they'd been dragged down the street by a giant bus.

"Maybe we should give the boiler a look too. It's been chugging along on empty for quite some time now," Leland said.

"Don't expect miracles. I'm just here to move the air around."

Near the back was a door that had been hammered shut long before Leland ever thought of buying a raunchy hotel. Clarissa mounted the steps and went to work. She placed her sage ball in the shell and lit it with a giant match. Instantly a small trail of smoke filled the air.

"Now, it's important we bring Mrs. Dauer into our thoughts and hold them with a light touch."

Devon and Leland closed their eyes and did their best to conjure up the bedraggled soul of the woman living in room 316.

"Her pain rides through this hotel, and we need to do our best to overcome it," Clarissa said.

Leland breathed until he could easily envision Mrs. Dauer in his mind's eye. With ease he saw her thick wintry coat and her wide stubby glasses and thought about the smidgens of food she undoubtedly had stashed away in every corner of her room.

"It's important we think of it as an offering and not a remedy," Clarissa said, closing her eyes and holding her shell directly above her head. "And we simply want to scent the air without lacquering it." She glided down the steps and through the back of the hotel with a faint ball of smoke hanging over her head. "And it's important there isn't a lot of talking. We'll let the sage do its work and we have to remember we're only along for the ride."

Around the boiler, Clarissa lingered a bit longer than with the rest of the basement.

"Tell me what you think is here, don't be shy," Leland said.

"Actually the boiler seems quite healthy. It's chugged along over the years quite nicely."

"Metaphors abound, don't they," Devon said, staring at Leland with a bright smile on her face.

"You might want to consider getting rid of some of this luggage. You're carrying quite a load down here."

"Maybe that's the next step," Devon said.

"We can load up the truck and make a run to the dumps," Leland said.

"Letting them sit in the desert would be nice but that's probably not appropriate."

On the elevator, they headed for the second floor.

"I don't want anyone thinking the place is on fire, so like I say, we'll only smudge the air."

Clarissa moved down the hallway, a mere messenger to the cloud that trailed out in front of her. Leland and Devon followed behind, quiet but earnest worshippers.

"Should we do your room?" Clarissa asked.

"Why not, we could use some help in there," Devon said.

"We all need help on occasion."

"And give the sheets a good little dousing while you're at it," Devon said with a different kind of smile on her face.

Clarissa did as she was asked, lightly smudging the door and window and giving the bed an extra layer of smoke. "I see things have been a little dormant in through here."

"I prefer to think of it as a respite," Devon said.

"We better hurry. Carly can't keep Mrs. Dauer in the lobby forever," Leland said with a whispery tone to his voice.

Upstairs it was more of the same, smoke and a ream of good thoughts.

"People are a little happier up here. I guess having no one living over the top of them is a big help."

"Two floors are enough to worry about," Leland said.

"Okay, onto Mrs. Dauer's room," Devon said.

Leland reached into his pocket for his passkey and opened the door. They were greeted by something more than a roomful of smells.

"Oh my, it's quite heavy in here, isn't it?" Clarissa said.

"Okay, let's give it all you've got," Leland said.

"She's so sad, it's unbelievable what she's had to carry over the years."

"No wonder she burrows through the trash," Devon said.

"She feels guilty, that's for sure," Clarissa said.

"Maybe she's done something awful in her life."

Clarissa shook her head. "No, it's more than the burden of others. Her father's spirit is everywhere in this room."

"Let's see if we can smoke him out," Leland said.

Clarissa relit her sage and let the thin trail of smoke do the talking for her. Around the dresser and through the closet, she held the burning bundle above her head until a heavy scent hung in the air. Finished, she turned and nodded, "I think we got it."

"Now it's time for the spirit of smoke to do its thing," Devon said with a snap of her fingers.

Leland and Devon walked Clarissa out the back and scurried off to the safety of their room and settled into bed. Sometime around three, Devon gave Leland a little nudge in the ribs. "Can you feel it, that scent is still in the air."

"I think so," Leland said, rolling over and breathing the best he could.

"I sure do," Devon said, nuzzling Leland and nibbling him on his ear.

"That sure is nice."

"How about we give new meaning to the word nice?"

Leland greeted Devon with a kiss and from there it was all smoke and memory and whatever he could bring with him from their first night together. Turning on the charm, she wandered and pursued the length of him, calling on high mountain streams and birds sitting along the fence line.

Devon finally let go with a tender gasp, "I love it when the air is just right."

§

Still in a soothing mood, Devon lay in bed and stretched. "Oh, what a night to remember."

"Clarissa seems to know her stuff, let's hope it works."

Before they could say more, the phone rang.

"Let me get it," Devon said, standing up and holding the receiver to her ear. "Oh, that's wonderful news. Thank you so much for calling."

She hung up and stared at Leland. "Guess what, that was the man from the appliance store. He said the stove will be in early next week. He even apologized for the delay. Said there was some sort of mix-up with the wholesaler."

"About time, if you ask me."

"Maybe it was the smoke."

Leland shrugged.

"I keep telling you, Clarissa knows what she is doing."

After last night's romp with Devon, he wasn't about to say anything. And before he could even ponder his decision, a loud knock on the door silenced the room.

"That's probably Carly wanting to know if we're still alive," Leland said.

He opened the door to find one very grumpy-looking Mrs. Dauer standing in the doorway. "I have a sneaking suspicion you tried to put a fast one over on me last night," she said.

"Me, what did I do?"

"You think I'm falling for that ruse about my grandson. That has to be one of the cruelest things ever done to anyone."

"I don't have the slightest idea of what you're talking about."

"I believe you were in my room last night and stunk it up with the worst-smelling perfume I've ever smelled in my life."

"Mrs. Dauer, please. Devon and I were fast asleep last night."

Devon stepped in between and gave Leland one of her nasty looks. "Careful with the lying," she said, barely above a whisper. "Mrs. Dauer, there's been a misunderstanding here. How about we look into this and get back to you?"

"I strongly suggest you do."

Closing the door, Devon turned and said, "That certainly puts a different spin on the morning."

"She's sharper than I thought."

"But we can't be lying to get ourselves out of this or we'll spin backward even more this time."

"I don't know what to do," Leland said, sitting down on the bed.

"Let's hurry up and do nothing."

§

After work Devon slinked through the door with a frown on her face. "I've been thinking we might need to bring Clarissa back for another round of smoke."

"I don't want to do that. I'll figure out a way to clean it up."

"But no more lying. This place can't afford it."

"You know I wrote her a letter once before and that seemed to help."

"But you have to tell her the truth."

"And telling her that it's her soul that has set the Eleanor on its heels could destroy her. So if I do fib, I'll keep it to a minimum. Besides, if you lie with good intentions, is that really a lie?"

"You just went deep on me with that one."

In the morning, Leland greeted Carly in the doorway.

"Look who's up and about at the crack of dawn," she said.

"I need some stationery and grab me a pen, if you will. I've got some things to tend to."

"Have you seen Mrs. Dauer? I thought she was going to rip my head off when I first got here."

"She knocked on our door and we tried talking to her but we'll probably have to do it again."

"And what do I tell the others about the smoke? More than a few around here are pissed off."

"Let 'em breathe, is what I say."

§

Nestling into his garden, he pulled his pen from his pocket and let the alluring page swim before him. Seeing his lies wander into the past would be freeing, he thought, if only he knew how. Messing with the truth was a glorious

find, and for a brief moment Devon's devotion to it held
him in its grip and he finally saw it as one of the great
vulgarities, something akin to staying inbounds at all times.

Dear Mrs. Dauer,

Please know that my daughter,
much to my chagrin, began
suffering hallucinations last night.
Her first flight-of-fancy happened
when she was only seven years old.
She came to us and declared that I
was a general in the Confederate Army
and that Union soldiers were over the
next rise. Naturally we rushed her to
the nearest hospital. Since then it's been
one outrageous episode after another,
given that we have no way of knowing
if your grandson was here or not.

In terms of the air freshener, we just happened
to be trying it out on the evening that Carly
chose to venture off into space. Trust me,
there was no connection between the two
events. What we sprayed into the air was called
Grey-Da-La-Mist, a new product on the market.
Each can sells for $7.85 and we have to buy four
cans to make the order complete. For that reason alone, we
have to be careful before we
commit to it with all our hearts. As of now
some of the guests prefer it, while others think
of it as nothing more than smoke gone array.

Please accept our most heartfelt apologies.

Signed,

Leland Powers
Owner/Operator
Eleanor Hotel

Downstairs he slipped his page of golden insights under Mrs. Dauer's door and walked away. In his room he found Devon still crimped beneath the covers barely awake but still warmly awash in her wholesomeness.

"How'd it go?" she asked.

"Went well, I think she'll understand we meant no harm."

"Did you lie?"

"Not much, I told her what happened was unlikely to ever happen again."

Slumping in his chair, he stared at the alley below him. All he saw was a raggedy old cat rummaging through the trash. He couldn't help but caress his means of communication tucked warmly away in his shirt pocket. Whether he put to use again or not, he knew his pen-and-ink overture was still riding firmly within him.

§

The overhead lights cast a hazy-like glow across the floor of the new café. Nevertheless, all of Leland's work shone through blissfully. The walls were rendered with softening tones of beige and white, and the linoleum floor glistened from never having been walked on by anyone but Leland, Carly, and Devon. But it was the stove that deserved all the reverence. A brand known as Wolf, a name that Leland deeply admired, sat firmly behind the counter, a manly display of steel cast in subtle shades of grey.

"I swear this café is going to sing," Devon said.

"It's something, that's for sure," Carly added.

"Next up is the menu, and once we get it figured out, we're good to go, we should be able to open sometime after the weekend."

"Whatever you ladies decide is fine with me. I'm ready to cook up some fine cuisine," Leland said, picturing himself standing over a bevy of pots and pans.

"I was thinking beef stew might be the way to go. I can even help prep if need be," Carly said.

"No, I've been musing over this, even dreaming about it. A full menu of vegetarian delights might put us on the map," Devon said.

"Mrs. Dauer eating kumquats and sprouts? I don't think so," Leland said.

"I don't think we should be promoting beef, it's too violent."

"How can it be violent? The cows are already dead," Carly said.

"My point exactly."

"These wackos wouldn't subsist on veggies if they were dipped in lard and covered with dollar bills."

"Carly, what did we say about sarcasm?" Devon asked.

"I know these people. Health and well-being aren't even in their vocabulary."

"Leland, do you mind weighing in here?"

"I'm not sure what to think," he said.

"I'm saying this is a long way to go to offer up some slop they can get up the street for a $1.98," Devon said.

"We don't have to offer up a pan of grease, but cucumber soup isn't going to cut it," Carly said.

"Please, can we let it be for now? But don't forget, I'm

going to be the one doing the cooking," Leland said.

"Okay, I didn't mean to go off like that. After all we are serving it up for free. You'd think they'd appreciate anything we had to offer them," Carly said.

"I plan on going to the bank today and moving some money out of my savings. For now all food costs will be on me," Devon said.

Despite the softening touch in both of their eyes, Devon and Carly had a mischievous way about them. High wisdom told Leland that trying to reason with either one was more than he could handle.

"I'll be on the roof if you need me," he finally said.

Not waiting for a reply, he turned and huffed his way out the door in what was his final word in what could have been an ugly fracas of the heart moving in the wrong direction.

With a pen firmly in hand, he tried shaking off the ill effects of the early morning spinout, but there was a chance the golden bliss of the other day with his lyrical homage to Mrs. Dauer was a onetime thing. He might well be one of those near poets whose only audience was a broken-down old woman with enough dust tucked beneath her eyes she could barely read.

Yet there was no reason to give up on his newfound love for poetry. Besides, seeing Carly in an ornery mood would most likely misplace him for the rest of the day, and he knew that Devon might be revving up her moody silence for some time to come.

So what he did was sit and let the early morning air work its wonders on his beleaguered heart and soul. Despite the coolness, he welcomed the briskness into his lungs and fashioned a thought that maybe the roof was his only domain. Maybe Devon could have his room and he could confine himself to the top of the hotel and do nothing else but tend to his garden. All he needed was a sleeping bag in one hand and a toothbrush in the other.

And that's how it happened. His pen and paper looked inviting for the first time today, and his clear liquid mind was upon him once again. As he took a final breath that bordered on the deep and the wonderful, his ink finally ran free.

Eat Fish

But think

About cows.

§

That evening Leland put forth his final word on the matter. "I have only one thing to say, catfish."

Devon looked at him. "Catfish, what the hell does that mean?"

"That's what we're serving up on opening night."

"Where did you come up with that one?"

"I think I've been dancing with the divine."

"Lay that on me one more time."

"There was something about that letter to Mrs. Dauer. Have to say, it got me going."

"She had an apology coming. We certainly weren't very nice to her."

"No, not that. It was the words. Something about the smell of ink."

"What's that got to do with catfish?"

"That's how I got the answer, by letting my pen open up and run freely."

"Oh boy, I hope you're not losing it."

"I'm more than fine. But it's about what we should be serving on opening night."

"Let me see it."

Leland pulled his crinkly piece of paper out of his shirt and handed it to Devon. She sat on the end of the bed and read his six words of poetic integrity. Like that her eyes widened and her mouth gave loose.

"You wrote this? Just now? Up on the roof?"

"I did, honest."

"And you didn't copy it out of a book, like one of those *Masters of Poetics Forms* I've seen around the library."

"No, ma'am, that's mine. I penned it while I was sitting in the garden."

Devon jumped up and pivoted over to the window. "You're more far-out than any brother could ever hope to be."

"You like it?"

"Like it, baby, I love it. It's got clarity up the yin-yang."

"So we're good with catfish?"

"Absolutely. In fact, I've got an aunt back home who has her own recipe for catfish. She won't even tell us where she got it."

"Let's get her on the phone. We open in a week."

"We've got to keep this in perspective," Devon said, sitting on the bed.

"Meaning?"

"Meaning, what happened on the roof wasn't only for you. We need to share it."

"How so?"

"Remember, we're not in the restaurant business. We're in the people business. They need to know there's a way of living that doesn't involve a ton of grease and five pounds of cigar smoke."

"You're losing me."

"These people need to read this before they take a bite. We can't have them slopping down a bunch of catfish without giving some thought to the violent world of cows."

"You sure about this?"

"That's what is so beautiful about this. We can't leap out of the gate yakking to them about sweat peas and cauliflower. We need to ease them into that realm, and this is how we're going to do it."

"So what's the next step?"

"The next step is going to the stationery store and buying some carbon paper. You need to be handing these poems out to everyone who can breathe."

Leland envisioned a day spent in splendor, him and his IBM Selectric, a worldly wordsmith basking in a river of his own making.

That afternoon it was type, type, and type some more. With each run-through, he assembled three sheets of stationery with two pieces of carbon paper in between. In all he wanted twenty sheets of poetic masterfulness to pass around to the folks in his hotel. Any more than that would be indulgent and he thought it was important to stay inbounds.

Finished, he took to the hallways, a chef brewing in his own art and most of all running on high. First up was Mrs. Dauer's door. Why not go to the heart of the matter, after all, it was her raging innards that had taken his hotel down into the bastion of terribleness. He taped his poem to her door and stepped back to admire it. To his way of thinking, it glowed like one of the neon signs up the street. From there it was onto Afra and Mr. Logan's way of living. They needed to know there was more to him than a basketful of tomatoes and a winsome look on his face.

The final coup d'état took place right there in the elevator, where most of the people in the hotel would see it and hopefully digest its meaning.

Stepping back he couldn't help but smile. Why not let the masses share in his poem? With luck it would be the first of many. Taping his finely crafted piece of work next to a panel that read First, Second, and Third floors, he read it one more time and then placed his fingertips to his lips and kissed the air. "Voilà," he said.

§

The door opened and in walked Devon. "We got that done. The kitchen is fully stocked and we're ready to go. Tomorrow night is going to be one hell of a gala."

Leland nodded like a prizefighter waiting for his big moment in the ring. "How many frying pans did you get?"

"Three, like you asked."

"That should do it. Catfish with string beans and a slice or two of tomatoes on top and French bread on the side."

"What about soup or salad, maybe even some dessert?"

"Nah, we're not that kind of place."

Back in the room, Leland announced his plans for the rest of the day. "I think I'll go upstairs and spend some time doodling with my pen."

"Best to get some rest, tomorrow is the big day."

The truth of the matter was that Leland had fallen in love with his calm, reflective way of living, and he needed the roof to ignite the warm glow of his juices that were all things creative. Staring at his garden, now nearly in full bloom, he knew it was a big part of the push forward, but pen and paper had opened a vein inside of him, most likely the same place where the hum had lingered for so long and ultimately called home.

Sitting in the same spot as the day before, he couldn't help but ponder what opening night was going to look like.

All the planning that he, Carly, and Devon had talked about was pretty good, but it was the rough ones that had his mind humming with a vigorous roar, the Dauers and the others like her who had fallen through the cracks. Maybe he'd been nothing more than a land baron filling up his pockets with fistfuls of pennies.

Now that he was riding high in the vigorous waters of his own creativity, he placed his head level with his paper and out came a ream of beats in perfect tandem with all the human hearts who were living beneath him.

Hotel Living

A hallway in a hotel.
A hot plate in every room.

Popcorn in the mouth.
Kernels behind the teeth.

§

The big night was upon them and Leland was a man riding high in style in nearly every way. Saggy T-shirt, firm-fitting Levi's, and a gray-and-white ball cap made him more than ready to fry some catfish. But it was the wisdom that he derived from penning his poem "Hotel Living" that really made him. The more he dabbed his catfish nuggets into a bowl of whipped eggs, the more he understood the link between his café and the garden and his pen. Since putting the finishing touches on his latest creation, he'd bought a notebook with his early morning sojourns in mind. He labeled it *Words Ready and Golden* by Leland Powers.

Afra, big and friendly, was the first through the doors,

followed by a weary-looking Logan and a couple of throwaways. "I have to see this to believe it. Leland cooking up a fine, fresh meal with us in mind."

"That's right, and it's going to be like this every night of the week," Devon said, standing next to her man in red slacks and a billowy white blouse.

"You know, most of us have never really had this," Afra said.

Leland turned and plopped his nuggets into a bowl of flour and nudged them back and forth with a giant fork. After they were thoroughly coated, he dipped them into a large frying pan sizzling with hot oil and left them there for at least three minutes. Finished, he patted them dry and served them up alongside a heaping pile of green beans.

Right behind Afra came Logan with a solemn look on his face. "I still haven't forgotten about the tomato that you tried foisting on me some time ago."

"From now on I'll see to it they're cooked."

"See that you do."

Next up were the faceless ones who drifted through the hotel colorless and alone, more apt to hole up in their rooms instead of the downstairs lobby. With them Leland only nodded and served, each time the spicy odor filling the air as he scooped more and more nuggets out of the pan.

"This way, gentlemen. We're serving family style and everyone will be sitting together," Devon said.

An hour into the festivities, Carly slinked through the door businesslike and calm with a big black ledger in one hand and a pencil in the other.

"What's with the notebook?" Leland asked.

"I've been going over the numbers. I want a ledger that shows me the last two years month-by-month. That way I can tell if we're doing all right or just holding our own."

"Father and daughter, both with their heads in the books," Devon said.

"Have you seen Mrs. Dauer?" Leland asked.

"I haven't, but I know she knows about it. She was in the lobby when a bunch of them were making plans to eat for free."

Like that she appeared, almost as if she'd been summoned, though there were no bugles announcing her arrival. But there she was, grimy and filthy and hunkered down in her long winter coat, staring at Leland through her overly thick glasses that made her eyes look like tiny slits filled with water.

"Nice to see you, Mrs. Dauer," Devon said.

"I figured you two earthlings would be serving smoked salmon," Mrs. Dauer said with a certain edge to her voice.

Leland and Devon caught the slur, but neither was in the mood to make a comeback.

"Would you like us to serve you up some food, or would you rather have a seat and we'll bring it over to you?" Devon asked.

"After you tried smoking me out of my room, I'm not sure I can believe anything you say. For all I know, you've got some arsenic up your sleeve."

"Mrs. Dauer, please. We're not out to hurt you," Devon said.

"What do you think that Dust-Da-La-Mist did to my lungs? I must have coughed for the rest of the week."

"Dust-Da-La-Mist, what the hell is she talking about?" Devon asked.

Leland motioned for Devon to join him behind the

counter. "In my letter, I told her we were trying out a new deodorant with the same name."

"So you're back to lying?"

"What was I supposed to say? We were trying to balance the energy in the hotel due to her tarnished soul?"

"Why not be honest for a change?"

"I'm hardly pathological, and we all know it."

"It better not be a pattern of behavior."

"And it's my job to keep the peace."

"Okay, let's go from here. Hopefully we can get her to eat something."

Devon stepped around the counter and sidled up to Mrs. Dauer. "Are you sure you wouldn't like a little something? Maybe a small slice of fish with some green beans and a tomato on the side and maybe a glass of milk to wash it down with? We'll gladly run up the street and buy a quart."

"Milk would be nice, it's been some time since I've had any."

"I'll run up to O'Dells, it will only take a second," Carly said.

"Mrs. Dauer, why don't you take a seat and we'll bring a serving over to you."

Mrs. Dauer did as she was asked.

"Are you sure you're up for doing this every night?" Carly asked.

"People have to eat every day, sometimes twice," Leland said.

§

Catfish gave way to chicken and that led to ham and of course tomatoes. Each was plump and ready to go, and to Leland's way of thinking, the crystals had done their job. On Wednesday it was fried rice with salmon on the side, and on Thursdays and Fridays, it was some of Thaddeus's potato soup, and the more that Leland stirred the pots and pans, the more he found what he was looking for. Spoons, knives, and splashes of milk were all part of his arsenal. He spent his mornings diving into his poems and his afternoons prepping for the big spread in the dining hall. Along the way images came and went. Starlight and strings. Mahogany and dust. Swimming pools and dogs, they were all part of the daily pursuit.

One morning, Leland and Devon slid the elevator open and he heard the loud shrieking voice that he knew absolutely belonged to his daughter.

"And I'm telling you what's done is done," she yelled loud enough to be heard around the block.

The recipient of this loud blast was a bald man with a polka-dot shirt and white leathery shoes. A battered suitcase sat near the door. Undoubtedly, he was one of the many guests staying in the hotel who never touched it in a deep and meaningful way.

"And I'll say it again, I barely slept last night because of the racket," he yelled.

"What's all the fuss about?" Leland asked in a booming voice.

"This gentleman had trouble sleeping last night because of Mrs. Dauer."

"Why, what did she do?"

"She kept me awake with her singing."

"What?" Leland asked.

Carly shrugged like it was difficult to understand what the man was talking about.

"You're telling me that Mrs. Dauer was singing last night?" Leland said.

"That's correct and it wasn't particularly great singing

either."

"She can barely breathe. Are you sure it wasn't the radio?"

"I'm telling you she was performing some sort of aria."

Leland glanced at Devon for help. "Must be the catfish."

"I know she had a second helping last night."

"I want something done about it," the man yelled.

"We'll talk to her, I promise you that."

"It's not enough. I want a refund."

"Sir, we don't operate like that. You had access to the room for nearly twenty-four hours, you must have gotten some sleep."

"And I'm telling you from midnight to four, I didn't sleep a wink."

"We live on the second floor and we didn't hear a thing," Devon said.

"And I'm telling you that this woman has got some pipes."

"I'll make sure I speak with her this morning. That's the best we can do."

The man leaned forward, nearly pinning his chest to the front of Leland's shirt. "And I'm not leaving until I get my eight dollars and fifty cents back."

"And I'm saying for the last time that there's no way in hell we're refunding any money."

"Then I'm calling the police."

Carly stepped in between the man and her father. "If you don't get out of here, we might be calling for an ambulance."

"Listen, girlie, I'm not someone you can push around with ease. I'll have you know, I used to box in college."

"And I used to drink like an orangutan."

"What the hell does that mean?"

"It means once I get started, I can't stop."

Now it was Leland's turn to unravel a notch or two. "If you don't leave right now, I'm going to toss you and your suitcase into the street."

"Try it," the man said, poking Leland in the chest.

Leland lunged and wrapped his arm around the man's neck.

"Now stop it, both of you," Devon said.

The slight twist of the man's neck must have snapped his mind back into place. "Okay, I'm leaving but I'm never coming back."

"Good!" Carly yelled.

The man straightened his shirt and headed for the door with his suitcase in hand. "You're all running some sort of flophouse here."

Leland took another step in the man's direction.

"Just let him leave," Devon said.

The man jostled out the door and disappeared around the corner of the building.

"What the hell do you think that was all about?" Leland asked.

"Maybe the guy is off his rocker," Carly said.

"Do you think Mrs. Dauer was singing arias last night?" Devon asked.

"I mean, he was emphatic about it," Carly said.

"Did anyone else complain?" Devon asked.

"Nope, not that I know of."

"Maybe you better have a talk with her," Devon said.

"I can think of other things I'd rather be doing."

Up in the hallway, Leland tried picturing Mrs. Dauer with her chest out and the high operatic words pouring from her mouth. Shaking his head, he knocked on her door, not knowing what to expect.

She opened on the second knock and stared up Leland with a blissful look on her face.

"The man next door was complaining this morning about you singing arias last night."

"I have to confess, I'm guilty as charged."

"So you were actually singing out loud?"

"I don't know what came over me. I was fast asleep and I woke up and I felt so warm and cozy and my stomach was so full that I started singing."

Leland felt a headache coming on, and he tried rubbing it away. "Have you always been a singer?"

"Not that I remember."

"Did you grow up around opera?"

"My mother used to have these albums. Caruso was a big favorite, but I don't ever remember her singing anything."

"What about your father? Did he like opera?"

Mrs. Dauer's face turned white and pasty. "Nah, he didn't like much of anything."

"Have to say this is a new one on me."

"Do you want me to stop, is that what you're saying?"

The businessman inside of him wanted it calm, if not downright quiet. But the emerging poet knew the value in exploration and discovery. "Keep it up, we'll get it figured out."

§

Leland was the first to tell the waitress what he wanted and that was a steak sandwich with French fries on the side. Carly followed up with a shrimp salad, and Devon asked for a bowl of vegetable soup.

"How's it feel to be back at the ShowCase?" Leland

asked.

"Seems like a thousand years ago, if you ask me."

"Maybe it has been. Just think of all the work you've done over the last year," Devon said.

"It's been damn hard at times."

"Nothing could be harder than what that fool put us through this morning," Devon said.

"You know, I was two ticks shy of knocking his block off," Leland said.

"Shouldn't get too mad, all he wanted was some sleep," Devon said.

"We still don't know how loud she was singing. Maybe it was barely above a whisper," Leland said.

"She's the last person I ever thought would be singing arias," Devon said.

"She said she rolled over in bed and felt so warm and comfortable that the music burst out of her."

"Wish that would happen to me. I'd love to sing an aria," Carly said.

Carrying plates in both arms, the waitress set all three orders on the table. Right behind her was a young woman in a green-and-white costume with a small tray tucked in the crook of her arm. "Keno, anyone?"

"No thank you," Leland said, shaking his head. For him gambling was the anthem of the swollen and defeated and the very reason the building they were sitting in was twenty-seven stories high.

"No, wait, let's play, you never know," Devon said.

"Yeah, let's mark a ticket," Carly said.

"I'll be right back," the keno gal said.

Devon grabbed a ticket out of the holder near the salt-and-pepper shakers. "No wait, we can't play, I forgot my purse."

"Let me get it," Leland said, fishing a pile of loose change out of his pocket.

"This is a first," Carly said.

Leland mumbled but said nothing more than that.

"Let's mark a 10-spot. If we win, we'll get twenty-five grand," Devon said.

"I see you know a little something about this," Leland said.

"I try my luck every year on my birthday. You never know, I might hit it big one of these years."

"That's the rally cry of every down-and-outer," Leland said.

"Let's do our birthdays," Devon said, picking up a crayon. "I'm June 7th, so I'll put a slash through the 6 and 7."

"I'm May 10th," Carly said.

"That's 5 and 10 and Leland is 11 and 8. That gives us 6, we need 4 more."

"Just pick any old ones, what does it matter," Leland said.

"No, it can't be random. It has to mean something. That's half the fun. I know, let's do Mrs. Dauer."

"I have no idea when she was born," Leland said.

"Let's make it up. What month do you think she was born in?" Devon asked.

Carly closed her eyes and wondered. "I say September."

"Good, that makes sense, so I'll mark the 9. Now we need the day."

"Number 1, what else? She was the number one topic of the day," Leland said.

"Perfect. That gives us 5, 7, 8, and 9, 10, 11, and 6 plus 1. Who knows, we might hit it."

"Two more," Carly said.

"I'll close my eyes and point," Devon said, quickly pointing at 67 and 72.

"Not a chance in hell," Leland said.

The keno gal swept by and swiped the ticket and two dollars and fifty cents off the table in one swift move.

"This is exciting," Carly said.

In all there were eighty numbers on the board and with each game twenty were called. That was cash money American style. The odds of pulling that off were about the same as hitting Mars with an air gun.

There were keno boards throughout the club, all synched up to the main counter not far from where they were sitting. The one they were fixated on was on the near wall less than twenty feet away.

"Showtime," Devon said.

The first number up was a 3, then came a 12 and a 22.

"Dang, nothing so far," Devon said.

"I could have told you that," Leland said.

In rapid fashion 6 and 7 flashed across the screen.

"There you go, we got 2," Devon said.

Leland barely gave the board any attention. Seconds later 27 and 29 hit but right after came 11, 8, and, 9.

"Look at that, we're gonna win some money," Devon said, barely able to speak.

"Well, I'll be," Leland said.

"Come on 1, 5, and 10," Devon screamed.

"This is like a horserace," Carly said.

As if on command, up shot the 5 and 10.

"We've got seven out of ten. That's $450," Devon said.

"I'll take it," Leland said, wiping his mouth with his napkin.

Then numbers 78, 79, and 80 swept across the board.

"Come on, Mrs. Dauer, give it to us good. Let's see number 1," Devon screamed.

And sure enough, somehow the old coot's number lit up the board. And right after came a couple of numbers that meant for nothing, then like that, like a flash of fire, 67 and 72 came into view. They'd done what only a few ever accomplished in the annals of gaming. They nailed a twenty-five-thousand-dollar keno ticket. Holy be to whatever, by Reno standards, Leland and company were now rich.

"Do you believe this?" Devon yelled.

"I'm about to wet my pants," Carly mumbled.

Both women turned and hugged like they'd been rescued off a desert island. Leland sat and stared at the numbers. The business side of him told him to count them one more time, which he did, and sure enough, out of the twenty called, they'd hit on half of them.

At the counter the supervisor verified the winning ticket. Soon after phones rang and other calls were made. Five men in suits appeared as if they had a mission in mind. Leland was asked to sign one paper and then another. At first his hand was steady and his penmanship pure, but by the last document, a slight tremor came upon him and he had to grab his fingers until they settled down.

"We should throw a party," Carly said.

"There will be no parties," Devon said before tipping her head from side to side. "Unless maybe it's a small one."

Leland slipped a check inside his pocket and pulled his coat tightly around him.

§

Devon curled in the middle of the bed and drew several heavy breaths. Leland pulled her close and gave her one mighty hug, but no matter how hard he tried, he couldn't close his eyes and drift off into the dreamy world of beyond. All the clamor about a keno ticket had worn Devon and Carly down into tiny numbs of fatigue. But for Leland, it wound him up until he thought that sleep was impossible.

Moving to his chair, he thought staring out the window might help with the rawness that was plaguing his stomach. At least there was a sliver of light shining through that might give him something to think about. Anything other than the money and the nonsense that had defined his day. In twenty-four years of operating the hotel, he had never once tussled with a customer, not even once. For sure there had been some loud screeches and firm demands, but he had never crimped his hand like he was ready to do battle.

Outside he fixated on a thrust of stragglers, three in all, wandering down the alleyway. One, two, three, like numbers on a keno board, they were there one moment and gone the next. That led him to thinking about the rooms in the Eleanor, all forty-nine of them, a number that had been with him for a good long time. How many to rent by the day and how many by the week, it was a ratio that had plagued him all these years.

The only thing he knew was to pick up his notebook and let his mind run wild and free. At first he relied only on circles to soothe the curious part of him, one on top of the other, five in all. Once he finished, the words began to flow.

Men with Ugly Hearts

Cause problems in the early
Morning dawn.

Sleeping is the only way in.

He found it swimming in its own power, without a doubt, more writing was the way to go. Finally Devon stirred and stared at him. "How long have you been sitting there?"

"Feels like a couple of years."

"Did you get any sleep at all?"

"Not much."

"Too keyed up from last night?"

"More than a little."

"Whoo-hoo, baby, we got some coins now."

"Looks to me like it's a blessing and a curse."

"What does that mean?"

"What the hell are we supposed to do with it?"

"I don't know. How about a rainy-day fund?"

"That would be part of it, but what's the other half of the equation?"

"Like doing something other than sitting here spinning our wheels."

"Is that how it feels?"

"Today it does."

"I thought we've been living our lives. I mean, look at all you've done to this place. You've got a garden, the café is coming along, and we get to cuddle in here most nights. I have to say we've been living right."

"But the numbers are off. The tourists are here on the weekends and we've got the high-flying acts to deal with the rest of the time. Maybe it's like you were saying about Mrs. Dauer before we smudged her room, we're still a little whacked around here."

"Hmm, this is a big one. I've been thinking we've been doing okay ever since Clarissa came in and did her thing."

"It's a mystery to me."

"You need some food in you. Sounds to me like you're running on empty."

Down the steps and nearly into the lobby, a tiny puff of light, the by-product of his poem, lit up his mind and folded the last piece of the puzzle into place. "I got it. No more misery for any of us."

Before he could finish his thought, he and Devon were standing in the lobby and Carly was leaning into the conversation.

"Look who's here, the millionaire."

"This millionaire has been up all night and needs a hot greasy meal to bring him back down," Leland said.

Devon opened the door and a gust of wind swept through the lobby. "We'll be right back, and if I'm lucky Mr. Leland will pick up the tab."

"Hold up a sec, let's have a little talk," Leland said, sitting down on the couch.

"Daddy, are you okay?"

"I'm fine."

"He's in the afterglow of yet another poem," Devon said.

"What's this one about?" Carly asked.

"This, the Eleanor, and what the hell we're doing here."

"We're trying to earn a living, or at least I thought so," Carly said.

"But then what? Maybe it's time we all gave some thought to what we're doing."

"And what the hell does that mean?" Carly asked.

"That bozo complaining about Mrs. Dauer singing an

aria. Who needs people like that?"

"What does that mean?" Devon asked.

"It means we don't need people like that clogging up the airwaves."

"But they're the customers."

"Who says we need customers?"

"How are we going to pay the bills?"

"We're rich, there's no need to sweat it."

"How do you figure?"

"Last night, we hit the big bonanza. Let's kick back and take it easy."

Carly spun around and pinned her face to her father's. "Have you gone completely bonkers?"

"Why don't we all just live here? Let's get rid of the tourists and the straight arrows and fill it up with some contemplative thinkers. You know, the ones that have got some soul tucked down in their bones."

"You mean only the down-and-out brothers and sisters can live here, and they're going to do it for free?" Devon asked.

"Why the hell not?"

"Oh baby, this is some sexy stuff you're laying down here."

"But what am I going to do? I need to earn a living," Carly said.

"We're going to pay you to keep order in the monastery."

"You mean I'm supposed to go head-to-head with a bunch of suspects?"

"We don't want that crowd. We want the reflective ones, the ones that have never fit in anywhere."

"But how are we gonna know who's who?"

"We have to interview them. We want only the

philosophical ones, everyone else can take a hike."

"What about the ones that are already here?"

"Some stay, some go. But we don't want sanctimonious do-rights even if they are on the quiet side."

"How about Mrs. Dauer?"

"She stays, of course. Anyone who can spin an aria is all right with me."

"What about Mr. Logan? He always pays his rent on time."

"You mean the guy who worked at the post office for 30 years and never said boo to anyone?"

"What the hell does that mean?" Carly asked.

"We only want the ones who went looking for it and never quite found it."

"This gets me going. I have to say whatever you do, don't stop writing poetry," Devon said.

§

Later that day, Leland, Carly, and Devon set about their plan, and Leland was the first to pitch in. "Remember, it's a two-step process. We have to determine who stays and who goes, and then we need to interview the incoming ones and decide who's right for the place."

Carly leaned back on the bed nearly nudging Devon in the side. "Are you sure you want to do this? There could be no coming back from a decision like this."

"We'll be fine. I've decided to sell my house, that will give us even more money to work with. Besides, I'll always be drawing a salary," Devon said.

"I've never been more clear about anything," Leland said from the comfort of his chair.

"He's been in the zone big time lately. The garden is coming along, and the poems simply won't quit. You should read some of them. And his cooking is getting better and better. I hear the compliments all the time."

"Have you given Mrs. Dauer a good look? I think she's put on weight. She's downright pudgy around the middle," Carly said.

Leland couldn't help but smile. There were no more drawing circles to get him warmed up in the morning. The words were coming, and he was doing his best to keep up. Flashpoints about planes and trains, not to mention hailstorms and large-sized mountains all dominated the landscape of his poetry. Some came clearly when he touched the tip of his pen to paper, others sprouted wings in his dreams and took flight the second he woke up. Soon he'd have to buy another notebook. In time he envisioned the top shelf of his closet filled with nothing else but poetry. Of late Devon claimed that every writer needed a magnum opus, and his needed to be entitled *A Man and His Garden—A Fragile Love Story*.

"But I don't know where to start," Carly said.

"We've got forty-nine rooms, and right now twenty-five are rented to regulars. Most likely five or six are going to have to hit the road. That means we'll have to interview thirty new people to fill up the place," Leland said.

"You want me to go out and find thirty new people to live here?" Carly asked.

"Not all at once. We need to make sure they're right for the Eleanor. We don't want any maniacs, I can't stress that enough."

"We need to put out the word and that means we start at the level of truth, cab drivers and bartenders. They're the only ones who ever really know what's going on," Devon said.

"You gotta like that," Leland said.

"How about the Holy Order? Are there any ladies

over there who would be a good fit for the Eleanor?" Carly asked.

"We might have one. She's older and she's recently finished her stay. She might enjoy living with us."

"But is she one of us? Has she looked into the Mystery and never been the same since? That's what we need to know," Leland said.

"She's a drunk, of course, she's done some of that," Devon said.

"So has she made it to shore or not, or is she still dithering around in the ethers?"

"She gave it a good run. She used to drink and try shampooing all the cats in the neighborhood."

"Did it work? Leland asked.

"She got arrested for trespassing."

"That's beautiful. See if she's interested."

"But the people we ask to leave, where are they going to go?" Carly asked.

"We want a smooth transition. We're not going to bounce anyone out on their ear. In fact I'm going to talk to Murray. Maybe some can move up to the Empire with him."

"I like Murray, he was a nice man. Maybe he'd like to move back in," Carly said.

"He did try and stage a revolt here, you gotta like that."

"But do we want people who have jobs?" Carly asked.

"Not our first preference, but there are always exceptions," Leland said.

"And Carly, what about you? Would you like to move in here with us?" Devon asked.

"Me here twenty-four hours a day? I don't think I'm up for that. I like my place. I like having a patio."

"Healing takes time, we all have to recognize that," Devon said.

§

Overnight Leland made up a list of all twenty-five guests living in his hotel on a weekly basis. Alongside each name, he added a mini-bio, who they were and what they did, and most importantly, if they'd idled their life away. If they had, he penned a tiny star next to the number of their room.

In the morning he and Carly walked through each one. Some were friendly but a few were nothing more than that. Most likely those were the ones that would have to go. The ones worth saving were busboys, fry cooks, even porters.

"We start with Logan. You're going to have to do this, after all, you're in charge these days, but I'll be there to help you."

"Are you sure you want to evict him? He's never caused any problems here."

"My point exactly."

"Are we going to knock on his door and tell him to get out?"

"We're going to sit him down and explain we're taking the hotel in a new direction, and there's a good chance he can move in with Murray. They have plenty of vacancies."

"Where are we going to do this? We can't evict people right here in the lobby, not in front of everyone."

"We'll set up an appointment for later today. I'll have a small table and a few chairs in the café. That way we'll have some privacy."

Around ten Leland gave Logan's door a hearty knock. Needless to say, he answered right away. "We're hoping you'll sit with me and Carly sometime this afternoon. We've got some new plans for the Eleanor and we want to bring you up to speed on everything."

"What the hell does that mean?"

"We'll explain it when the time is right."

"I hope you're not going to get the smell campaign going again. You damn near drove us crazy with that nonsense."

Leland had hardly given up on the smell. When he sensed it was wise, he planned to suit up and give it another go. "No, we're not going to trot out the soapy water. We'd appreciate it if you'd meet us in the café in about an hour."

Leland scurried downstairs and set up a small table and chairs in the center of the café. From there it was onto the vegetables and his daily round of chopping and preparing for tonight's big dinner, which was chicken tacos laced with celery.

At 12:45 he and Carly were sitting in their chairs ready to give Logan the once-over.

"I hope he doesn't get mad," Carly said.

"How about we tell him the next couple of weeks are on the house? That ought to soften the blow."

"What if he starts crying?"

"I doubt he's got much water in him."

At precisely one o'clock, Logan walked into the café. His stride was short but tentative, like he was convinced there was a giant sinkhole waiting to gobble him up. "Are you trying to recruit me to chop vegetables? Is that what this is all about?"

"Not exactly," Carly said.

Mr. Logan sat down across from her and her father.

"After a lot of contemplation, we've decided we're going to do something new and different here at the Eleanor. We're going to stop renting to people on a nightly and weekly basis. We want more of a homey atmosphere,"

Carly said.

"What's that got to do with me?"

Carly grabbled to find the words she was looking for, so Leland stepped in. "We're going to stop collecting rent altogether. We're looking for a certain type, and you don't fit the profile."

"What the hell is a profile?"

"You're comfortable in life. You have your finances in order. We'd like people who have danced along the edge and never quite recovered."

"You know, the warrior class. The type of people I've always been in love with," Carly said.

"You're evicting me? Is that what I'm hearing?"

"Not exactly. We just don't want you living here anymore."

"What the hell is the difference?"

"We would appreciate it if you'd move up the street to the Empire. Do you remember Murray? He said you're more than welcome up there."

"But you can't kick a guy out for no reason."

"In Nevada, you can," Leland said.

§

After sifting through various names and sizing people up, Carly finally synced up with her father's way of thinking. Gone was the bartender who liked to go on and on about the Yankees but jeered every woman who walked through the lobby. Also asked to leave was the man from Massachusetts who liked to drink and yell at the pigeons on the ledge outside his window. In was a man who was born to blind parents but found refugee shelving books in the local library and reading about the origins of glass. Also allowed in was an usher from down the street who liked eating popcorn and listening to the radio every night after work. But after three weeks of sifting through the list of hopefuls, the Eleanor had not fully transitioned into a temporal space.

"I've got two more coming in this afternoon," Carly said to her father.

"So far so good, if you ask me. A lot of the new ones have that faraway look in their eye that I've admired for a long time."

"But do you know how many people I've turned away? It's endless. Wifebeaters, convicts, silly-looking priests, and partying students. I mean, the word is out all over downtown, free rent in exchange for quiet reflection. But most people don't have a clue what I'm talking about."

"Figures."

"At least we've got the cat lady coming in, the one Devon talked about. I don't think we need to vet her."

"Just tell her to leave the shampoo at home."

"How about Logan? He's been dragging his feet."

"I placed a couple of empty boxes outside his door last night, that ought to wake him up."

"He doesn't even speak to me anymore."

"Devon has come around to my way of thinking. She thinks as soon as we get rid of him, we'll tick even further up the ladder."

"I still think he's a nice man," Carly said.

"We don't need anyone around here who covets canned tomatoes."

"But what if we guess wrong and some of the people aren't as reflective as we think?"

"Then we'll dump their asses. If I'm going to write every morning, I need it quiet."

"Do you plan on doing anything with these poems?"

"I plan to start my garden poems next week, no telling

where they'll take us."

"If you say so."

"Lately I've been contemplating the relationship between a seed and a skyscraper. This could be the one that is going to take us on a ride."

Shortly after two, the door opened and a tall gangly man with a bald head came ambling in the door.

"This is the next one up, I think he's going to be good."

"Is it all right if I join you?" Leland asked.

"Sure, why not?"

The man said his name was Anthony, and he spoke in a serene way, which Leland admired. The three of them sauntered down the hallway to the café. Leland noted that the man's hands were soft and tender to the touch. That was a good thing, he figured. Indoor people were more likely than the outdoor ones to help him realize his dream of livng in a cozy place.

"Is this the café where people eat for free?"

"It is, my father is turning out to be quite the cook."

"Impressive."

"So how did you hear about us?" Leland asked.

"A dishwasher I know mentioned it. I believe he spoke with you the other day," he said, pointing to Carly.

"That was Terrance. He didn't quite work out. He's on a bowling team. That's not what we're looking for."

"You don't like the sport?"

"It was all the talk about his trophies. He asked if he could display them in the lobby."

"Apparently there's some talk about whether he earned them or went out and bought them, if you know what I mean."

"Nice," Leland said.

"I don't want a bunch of bowlers hanging around the lobby," Carly said.

"But what if they're pretend bowlers?" Leland asked.

"Not for me."

Leland cleared his throat. "So Anthony, what can you tell us about yourself?"

"I bus dishes at the El Matador. I've been there for quite some time. I have to say, I enjoy it there."

Leland gave Carly one of those what the hell is going on kind of looks. She knew he frowned on steady employment. Being as discreet as possible, she leaned into her father and said, "But he has a PhD."

"Oh, I see, that's different. So you graduated and took a job downtown busing dishes?"

"I got my degree about twelve years ago, and then I saw an ad in the paper for busboys, so I thought I'd apply."

"Isn't that something? So, what is your degree in?"

"Philosophy. I like the Greeks. I've always been very fond of *The Republic*."

"So you're still studying?"

"Without question. There's a very interesting line of critical thinkers that I find fascinating."

"So you're reading all the time?"

"That's what I do, I read and bus dishes."

"Anything else?" Carly asked.

"Not that I can think of."

"Absolutely beautiful," Leland said.

"So I'm in?"

"I don't know why not," Leland said, staring at Carly for confirmation.

"I knew he'd be good."

"Would you like a room with a view or one of the darker ones on the south side?"

"A dark room seems good to me."

§

By July the three pursuers of peace and calm were spending more and more mornings before Devon scurried off to work lounging around the rooftop in broken-down chairs that Leland had found abandoned in the alley. Not far away was the garden by now fortified by Clarissa's crystals and beaming with tomatoes just shy the size of softballs and always a part of the nightly staple in the café.

"I wake up every morning and can't wait to get up here," Leland said, fondling his notebook.

"I hear that," Devon said.

"Who would have thought that sunshine could be so good for someone?"

By now the hotel, if one could even call it that, was the happy domain of sleepy time bliss. With little ceremony or any kind of outrage, Leland dismantled the "No Vacancy" sign and tossed it into the trash. Next up were the ledgers, deposit books, and any other references to financial outlooks that he confined to the deepest parts of the company safe. The only remnants from the hotel itself were the registration cards. Leland felt it was important to know who was who and who belonged where. But one thing for sure, the old days of Johnny Do-Rights from California yelping about the glory of 77 cent breakfasts while refugees from the back hallways were screaming and hollering about chipped tile in the bathrooms were over. In their place was a band of loners dedicated to a near code of silence from one day to the next.

Oh, sure, there were problems. Turns out that Anthony, the philosophical busboy was a very dark cloud instead of being one of the contented dropouts Leland and Carly had hoped for when they first sat him down for an interview. His sullen and faraway looks were the cause of worry to some, but Leland came to his rescue by proclaiming, "We all find it in our own way, best to leave him alone."

But beyond Anthony's moody indifference, Carly had done her homework and filled the rooms with chronic outsiders dedicated to the delicate winds of interior silence. Leading the way was Jerry Mayweather, a cop who'd been fired for falling asleep in the park alongside a bevy of roses. After him came a dethroned sorority mother who nearly drank herself to death after finding out what boys and girls did in the bushes right under her bedroom window.

"And most of all, Carly, we have to say thank you. You helped us pull off the transition," Devon said, stepping onto the elevator.

"I know I wouldn't have been up for a string of interviews like that. Just think, one or two slip-ups and we could have a bunch of terrorists on our hands," Leland said.

Carly was dressed in Levi's and a tight-fitting T-shirt and was soaking up the praise as if she was standing behind a podium at a college graduation. "That was interesting, to say the least. To think of all the people that are out there hanging on by their fingernails."

"We call them the invisible people. I'm thinking of writing a poem about them," Leland said.

"One was a deaf-mute who wanted to raise squirrels in his room. Can you imagine the smell? And then there was the embittered mailman who said he liked playing darts without a dartboard, if you get my drift," Carly said.

"You mean he was planning to pepper the walls with tiny holes? That's something to think about. He can't be all bad."

"I'll put him on the waiting list."

"I have to say since we did this, I've never slept better in my life," Devon said.

"What we need is a celebration," Leland said.

"We're already cooking them dinner, what more do they want?" Carly said.

"Tonight is the first night that all forty-nine rooms are filled with the kind of people we've been looking for," Leland said.

"Hear, hear to that," Devon said.

"Maybe we need to thank them for being here," Carly said.

"You've gotta like that," Devon said.

"How about we have everyone assemble in the lobby after dinner and we simply say welcome home," Leland said.

"Maybe we need a poem to celebrate the occasion," Devon said.

"I'd be up for that. Anything that keeps my pen alive and well."

"You better start cracking, we serve dinner in ten hours," Carly said.

"Showtime is upon us," Devon said.

§

Luckily all of his peas and beans had been washed and cleaned in preparation of the evening salad. Later that day he would debone the trout and coat every one of them in flour. His only task at hand was his welcoming poem, and now that his hotel was filled to the very brim, he knew that his pen was the savior of his soul and nothing else.

The Cave Is Where You Ought To Be

What is this dark cave
That has come upon us?

Doorways and hallways
And elevators that barely work.

Rooftops covered in snow
Must live within the breath.
Noses and throats help
Lead the way.

He sat and read his poem, and somehow it blew through him with ease. Closing his notebook, he thought only of the nearby mountains. Where would he be without them? The thin divide was nothing more than a puff of smoke.

Downstairs he prepped for the evening meal, forty-eight hungry souls plus Devon and Carly. The muscles needed were very different than the ones he used for his hotel. There it was a daily tussle of monies and rent. Life in the café was a daily performance, every meal a poem of sorts.

By five-thirty the housemates began trailing in, among them Afra and Mrs. Dauer. Right behind came the threadbare and thoroughly debunked officer, Jerry Mayweather, a master at pretending to need the Thorazine shuffle to find his way. Dressed in fading slacks and a white shirt, he requested only vegetables, saying a hot and simmering piece of fish was not to his liking. According to Carly, it was the quota of having to pull over seventeen people per day that was more than he could bear, hence his need to sleep in the park.

Devon and Carly were some of the last to arrive,

chatting back and forth like little schoolgirls on the playground.

"Why don't you join us, you must be famished," Devon said.

Leland stepped back from the frying pan. He hadn't taken the time to chow down himself.

"Do you want to ask everyone to assemble in the lobby or should I?" Devon asked.

"Why don't you do it? They'll respond more to your voice than they will mine."

"Why don't you simply thank everyone while they're sitting here?" Carly asked.

"The lobby is where we hum, let's do it there," Leland said.

Carly didn't fight back. After all, she was in charge of who came and went, her father was an ethereal presence who floated by with a pen in one hand and a spatula in the other.

"Everyone, please can we have a moment of your time? We're hoping we can gather in the lobby, Leland has a few things he'd like to say. Many of you may not know it, but this is the first time since we locked up the cash drawer that every room in the Eleanor has someone living in it."

Normally one would think a quiet cheer would overtake the place, but this band of discards and throwaways merely stared at Devon with a sea of questioning eyes. Knowing them, they probably thought they were sitting on top of a giant sinkhole that was about to give way at any moment.

"Just leave your plates and dishes here. We'll gather them up later," Leland said.

"I'll do it. You've had a long day," Carly said.

One-by-one his gathering of darkly divided souls

slithered into the lobby. And never once in the history of the hotel, had Leland tried squishing fifty-one guests into the lobby at one time.

But somehow it happened. Three men found comfort in the middle of the couch. One fellow, a broken-down cab driver, who only drove once a week, sat on the floor and others quickly followed his lead. The final accomplishment came when a bundle of men filled the first few steps leading up to the second floor. Sitting in the big overstuffed chair next to the counter was Mrs. Dauer, regal now that her belly was filled with fish and an array of vegetables that Leland and Devon and handpicked from the store.

"I don't want to take up too much of your time but on behalf of myself, Carly, and Devon, we would like to thank you for joining us here at the Eleanor. As Devon mentioned, this is the first night that all forty-nine rooms have been occupied under this new agreement to pursue the collective silence."

"We hear that," a tall fellow that Leland barely knew yelled from the back row.

"To honor the evening, Leland has a poem he'd like to read," Devon said.

Leland pulled his notebook out from the shelf next to the safe. Luckily he remembered to earmark his work with a slip of paper so it was easy to find.

Never once thinking of himself as a public performer, he had to let the words find their way so the rhythms could highlight what he had to say. "I call it 'The Cave Is Where You Ought To Be.'"

His assemblage of desperadoes stared at one another like they had no idea what he'd said to them. It had never occurred to him that many of them wouldn't know a poem if they passed it on the street, let alone what it was supposed to sound like. But of course he hoped he had Anthony, his fellow contemplative, on his side. Needless to say, he would know what a poem was up to when it was read aloud. But being the intellectual he was, his standards were up there with Homer and no one else, so Leland didn't know if he would be on his side or not.

The first few words sputtered out of Leland's mouth like he'd never spoken in his life. But by the time the image of the hallway came into view, he hit his stride. Each well-honed phrase was like a small hill that needed to be negotiated but he did so with ease. At one point he stole a glance at his lovely Devon. She was standing close by softly aglow in the splendor of every word that spewed forth from her boyfriend's way of speaking.

His final offering of "lead the way" blew out of his mouth like pearls on a string. He raised his head and moistened his lips. Triumph comes in many forms and this was one of them.

At first Leland had to face one terrifying moment of silence, different from the one he'd been hoping for. This was more like a thumbs-down and he began questioning his abilities to run a poem across a piece of paper. But to his glory, Anthony jumped up and pranced like an Indian around a campfire late at night. Soon after his fellow roommates let loose with a hearty but undisciplined show of support, clapping and hollering until their voices rose up and floated out of the hotel and into the air surrounding them.

Leland stood there firmly on display, knowing this was his one and only public display of what he thought of as his wonderful words of knowing how to live. He felt no need to bow and scrape or take on an endless stream of compliments. Instead he quietly watched his fellow inmates disperse up the steps in a single line and back into their rooms.

"You brought it home this time," Devon said, rubbing his back with the palm of her hand.

Upstairs he flopped into his chair. He had no idea the reading of a poem could be so exhausting.

"I bet I sleep tonight. Besides, I have an appointment with the realtor first thing in the morning," Devon said.

"Are you sure you want to follow through with that?"

"Absolutely. We can't run this place on money from a keno ticket."

"We're in this for a good long haul, aren't we?"

"Making it up as we go along. I've been doing that since the day I was born."

He stood up and paced around the room. Living as freely as Devon did not come as easily to him. He'd always needed the daily quest to unfold in front of him so he could go charging through the day.

Shedding his work shirt and clad only in his dungarees, he was suddenly overcome by the events of the day. His breathing fluctuated, and he dropped to one knee, wedging himself between the bed and the nearby sink. He stared up into the inviting face of his loving girlfriend, knowing she'd been shaped and honed by the wisdom she sustained from running the Holy Order all these years.

"Marry me," he said, refusing to let any anguish or schoolboy neediness seep into his voice. After all, he was a public poet who knew something about stature and solemnity.

Devon stared at him and ran her fingers across the top of her head. For a second, he thought she was lost somewhere inside of herself, but the fear didn't linger for long.

"Of course, I'd be honored to be your wife."

Standing, he held her and pulled her close. Kissing her once, twice, even three times, he knew he would be cuddling with her all through the night.

§

In the morning Leland was on the phone. After an easy go with Devon, they both agreed that Thaddeus was the right man to perform the nuptials. Before they ran him up the flagpole, there'd been some talk about having Clarissa come in and light them up with smoke and fire, but Leland wasn't in the mood to be bewitched.

Thaddeus was a man of the soil and therefore right for the job. On the third ring, he answered and Leland gave him the news. "Guess what, I've asked Devon to marry me."

"Well, what did she say?"

"Of course she said yes."

What followed was a series of yelps and cheers, and there was not a single question about the color of Devon's skin. What was there was Thaddeus's desire to please.

After Leland hung up the phone, Devon announced, "I'm thinking if we're going to get married, we need to go buy some clothes. We can't be showing up in our regular go-to-work outfits."

"A new suit might be in order."

"And maybe you should think about getting a haircut," Devon said, rubbing her hand across the back of Leland's head.

Leland's hair was dovetailing over the back of his collar and partway down his neck, and it had never been this bushy. "I'm not in the mood for sitting around a barbershop, the hell with it."

"What, then?"

Ever since he had penned his first poem, pondering took on a whole new meaning for him. It was as if his new way of living had opened into a whole new realm of thinking clearly.

"Western wear, that's what we need."

"Say that again."

"I'm talking about cowboy clothes."

"Are you out of your fucking mind? I can't be wearing cowboy clothes. I'm from the Bronx, you can't dress me up like some square."

"We live in the West, don't we?"

"But me in cowboy boots, you have to be kidding."

"What's it going to hurt?"

Devon wiggled back and forth and gave Leland an impish smile. "You know, I did see a stylish pair the other day in a magazine."

"That's it, let's go get them."

"I'll say one thing, you sure the hell ain't boring."

Sam's Western Wear was up the street nearly three blocks away. Leland and Devon hightailed it up there in less than five minutes. Inside it was Levi's, blue jeans, and tall mirrors. The only thing missing were some cows and a bale of hay.

"Can we help you?"

Standing before them was a man with imposing shoulders and a belt buckle containing enough silver, it could be mined for a healthy dollar or two.

"We're here to do a little window shopping," Leland said.

"Help yourself, there's plenty to choose from."

Leland and Devon brushed past him without saying anything more, but both caught the lingering look of disdain in his eyes. They both knew by now that black and white combos didn't play well in all parts of downtown Reno.

"I don't think we'll be sitting down to dinner with him anytime soon," Devon said.

"Not if I can help it."

Near the rear of the store was a long ream of shirts, some plainer than others but all aglitter with buttons in a wide range of reds, greens, and blues.

"Those are marrying clothes if I ever saw any," Leland said.

"But me looking like a cowgirl, I'm not sure about that."

"We need a look that everyone can relate to."

"As long as I like my boots, I guess we'll be all right."

Leland eyed a mannequin with a brown cowboy shirt with pearly white buttons that were more than a little bright.

"Look how silky it looks," Devon said, fingering the sleeves.

"You're welcome to try one on," a lily-white salesclerk said from behind the counter.

Leland thumbed through a stack of shirts and pulled one from the bottom that looked exactly like the one they'd been staring at. He disappeared into the dressing room and was back in less than a few seconds.

"Look what we've got here. If light brown isn't your color, then I don't know what is."

Leland stood in front of the mirror and preened from side to side, nodding his approval from every angle. "I think I need a hat," he said.

"Are you kidding me, you in a cowboy hat? Now that might be pushing it a bit too far."

"No harm in looking."

In the very center of the store was a full display of noggin wear. Some were made out of straw, others out of high-quality cloth, but there was one for everyone, young, old, and naturally big and tall.

Leland tried on a giant Stetson and stared into the mirror. "What do you think? Is it me?"

Devon saw how high the hat rode on him and more or less diminished the size of his head. "If that's you, then I sure the hell don't know who I've been sleeping with these many months."

Leland gave himself one last misguided look in the mirror. "Have to say, I kind of like it."

"But it doesn't like you," Devon said.

From there it was on to hats big and small and foisted up in a variety of colors. Some rode nicely and others not at all. None of them did much to highlight the deep and satisfying wrinkles in and around Leland's eyes that gave him that look of well-groomed integrity that Devon so deeply admired.

"I'm hoping this doesn't take all day. I've got boots to plow through."

"How about that one in the back?" Leland asked.

On the back row, smack dab in the middle, sat a brown derby hat that had the look of the early days in San Francisco right before the big quake. There was no doubt about it, it was much more city than country, and Leland found himself mesmerized to the very core of his being.

"Maybe, maybe," he said, slipping the derby on and immediately feeling the comfort it gave to all sides of his head.

"My, my, we might have something here," Devon said.

Leland gave it a firm tug and that more or less confirmed it was the one for him. He walked over to the mirror and checked himself from all angles and like what he saw, a western shirt and matching derby hat. He now looked exactly the way he hoped for, a weird mix of an Idaho farm boy and a man who breathed debits and credits until he finally woke up.

"Oh baby, that's so you. Dapper and debonair, yet homey and down-to-earth."

"We'll take it," Leland said.

"Now it's my turn."

The next ninety minutes were given over to Devon. Hoop skirts and billowy blouses were the order of the day. And to top it off, she eyed the lady's footwear on display near the front of the store. Large and small and red and white, and every color in between, all of them were given a chance to make it on their own.

"What do you think?" Devon asked, twirling around and sporting a pair of finely tailored black boots with slick polished leather and a little tab on the back of each one that made them easy to slip on every time she wanted to give Annie Oakley a run for her money.

Leland and Devon stood side by side more than ready to make their debut, him rustic and white, her ebony and finally western in every way.

§

Back in their room, the western wear went into the closet and stayed there for another week or so, while Leland and company took turns planning for the wedding. A menu went on display, prime rib with potatoes and big burly sprouts on the side. Carly stepped up and did nearly all of the cooking. No one needed a tired-looking Leland barely hanging onto Thaddeus's words when it came time to truly unite with Devon. And in terms of invitations flowing out to anyone outside of the Eleanor clan, they were virtually nil. The only exceptions were some of the gals from the Holy Order of Recovered Sisters, the ones Devon truly admired. Other than that, this was a family affair through and through.

On the day of the wedding, Leland was up early and took a shower. It was agreed upon that he wouldn't be writing any poems, at least not today. No one needed him being dreamy and somewhat detached when it came time to stroll down the aisle with Devon.

As for Devon, she went about her day differently. She vanished to the Holy Order and hid behind a voluptuous pile of paperwork and some serious sit-downs with two out of control women who had tested the limits of legality by speeding through the center of town in a Mustang convertible singing the Star-Spangled Banner.

"Are you all set?" Carly asked on Leland's first pass through the lobby later in the day.

"Pretty well settled that it's a go. A few days ago I was convinced that Devon was going to hightail it back to New York, so I had to take myself out for a walk until I could put my head back on straight."

"Did something happen? Did you two have an argument?"

"No, my nerves got the best of me."

At noon Thaddeus rolled up outside in his worn-out Chevy, wearing a huge grin on his face. Dressed in dungarees and a white shirt, he looked very much like an older brother on the prowl. He and Leland shook hands and went so far as to pat one another on the shoulder in a rare moment of public adulation.

On the inside it was all Thaddeus and Carly. She

smiled and gushed at the sight of her potato farming uncle whom she hadn't seen since her teens.

"I hear you're running this place now," Thaddeus said.

"Oh, I lightly steer it. It pretty much runs itself."

"Being in business has to be a lot better than working in the clubs."

Carly replied with a simple nod of her head. Thaddeus didn't know that the Eleanor was no longer a profit-eating machine but had been transformed into a cozy bunkhouse for misfits and weirdoes of the quiet sort of life.

"Come on upstairs and see the room. Devon will be back later on."

"She sure seems like a nice girl. We had the longest talk on the phone."

"I tell you she's been a delight. She's the reason that Carly is back up on her feet and doing so well."

"She certainly looks fine. I have to assume she's been taking care of herself."

"The best she's ever been and we have Devon to thank for it. They're almost like sisters. In fact we're going to have to put you up at her place. All the rooms here are taken."

"On a Wednesday? That's fantastic. I thought you only filled up on the weekends."

"We'll have to talk about that. There have been some changes here at the Eleanor."

In the room Thaddeus looked around and let his shoulders slump more than once. "The two of you are living together in this tiny little room? How do you stand it?"

"We like the coziness of it. We're not convinced a house would make us any happier than we are now."

"But where's the bathroom?"

"Right outside the door, exactly where it belongs."

"And Devon likes it like this?"

"Loves it, she's got more than a little moxie in her."

"But I mean, most women would like a house of their own, wouldn't they?"

"She's got a lot of the Bronx pinned down inside of her."

Thaddeus sat down on the end of the bed and bounced up and down. "So what's this about the hotel being filled up in the middle of the week?"

Leland stared at his brother and gulped like he did when he was a little boy. From there it was on to Devon and their magical nights of tender loving care and a winning keno ticket that seemed to have fallen from the sky. Next up was Mrs. Dauer and her rendezvous with the trash and finally how they decided to fill up the Eleanor and put a fine cooked meal on the table at the same time emphasizing that it was not about catering to hooligans and thieves but more for people who viewed life from the other side of the street.

Now Thaddeus, who'd been born and bred on the dark brewing thoughts of the *Book of Mormon,* didn't offer up any kind of rebuttal. He stood up with bewilderment in his eyes and no doubt there was some even hiding underneath the top layer of his skin, but he only shrugged and said, "You always did go your own way."

§

At seven in the evening, the two lovebirds dawned their highfalutin Western wear, her in her hoop skirt and him in his fancy shirt and a brown derby hat. They stepped into the elevator and rode it to the top of the hotel.

And from there it was onto the wedding, with Carly taking most of the credit for such a high and mighty performance. At the back end of the roof were four tables, each sitting twelve to thirteen people. All were covered with red-and-white checkered clothes and an array of silverware and tall drinking glasses. The only stipulation that Carly held firm to was that no alcohol was to be smuggled in underneath someone's jacket or tucked deep inside their back pocket.

"I don't see any reason to be milling around, do you? Let's get the show up and running," Thaddeus said.

"Let's go, I plan to be in bed by 10 o'clock," Leland said.

"Now, I've married a lot of people, but we usually start off with a little music."

"The simpler, the better is what I say."

Thaddeus proceeded to the spot that Carly had carved out for him not far from the elevator. Leland and Devon stood there and waited for him to get in place and give them a big hearty wave to start walking his way, which he did almost like signaling the start of a race.

In perfect unison, Devon and Leland began striding his way, Leland solemn and ready, while Devon walked with a lighter touch and sported a soft serene smile like she'd finally been rewarded with something she'd been waiting for a long time.

"Can I get everyone to stand and gather around?" Thaddeus said.

The band of stragglers followed suit, grouping in twos and threes and milling around like they were at a funeral. Even Mr. Dauer shook herself free from her tiny abode and joined the festivities, though she still wore her heavy coat in eighty-five-degree weather.

Carly stepped out of the crowd looking striking in a white cotton dress and a string of light-blue pearls hanging from her neck. In one hand she held a saucer from the café with a ring on it that Leland had bought up the street for less than two hundred dollars.

Thaddeus cleared his throat and said, "We are here to bring Leland and Devon together in perfect harmony with the world around them. We come to this with the full promise of the vows and what they mean to one another."

From there he prattled on about marriage being sacred and he didn't dare venture into the muddy waters of Mormonism or even Jesus Christ for that matter, all of this coming from Devon, who had been quite adamant about it when she and Thaddeus worked through all the details on the phone.

"Do you, Leland, take this woman, Devon, to be your loving wife to comfort and care for in both sickness and health from this day forward?"

Leland gave it his very best, "I do."

Thaddeus rolled over to Devon and let go with the same spiel, making sure he said everything in the same way. Devon responded with an "I do" that was firm and full of commitment.

Thaddeus motioned for Carly to step up to the front and present the ring to her father. Leland slipped it off the saucer and onto Devon's finger with utter ease.

"This ring symbolizes the unending virtue of this marriage forever and a day. I now pronounce you husband and wife. You may kiss the bride."

Leland leaned forward and gave Devon a kiss on the lips that surpassed all the others he had given her in the past. In return Devon was right there with him, letting her lips receive him without hesitation and accepting him until they were old and slobbering and saying to one another, how do I know you?

The ravenous band of hotel livers let loose with a wild and uproarious round of applause that every one of them pulled up from the bottoms of their bellies and spewed into the air. Leland quietly noted that the roar was richer than the one his poem had received but he told himself not to dwell on it, in time poets always have their day.

"Let's eat," Carly yelled, "And I want everyone to know that I cooked it myself, with Anthony pitching in from the side."

Anthony was right alongside doing his very best to keep his stoic manner sealed into place. Devon and Leland were asked to sit at the end of the biggest table, where Carly served up two platefuls of prime rib and all that went with it. Sitting next to them was Thaddeus looking proud and happy and not bothered one bit that he'd veered away from the teachings of Joseph Smith and Brigham Young.

Leland leaned forward and slipped a piece of juicy red meat into his mouth. Somehow he was feeling worn out. Pledging his love to Devon in front of so many people had taken some of the heft out of him. With his last bite, he stood up and stretched. Devon on the other hand seemed like she'd been enriched with fairy dust, smiling and joking with Carly and everyone passing by the table.

Not wanting to bother his newly found wife, Leland stood up and walked over to his garden. This year's crop was bountiful, surpassing last year's in sheer numbers and size. To help clear his mind, he wandered to the front end of the hotel and stared down at the sidewalk, one he had swept and cared for over the years. Turning he stared at the ongoing revelry. Thaddeus was talking to a young man who pedaled a bike and delivered papers by hand. Mormonism was most likely a part of the conversation. Carly wasn't too far away jabbering with one of the newly sober ones from the Holy Order, detailing the pitfalls of drinking and the gloriousness of showing up on time and knowing how to work. Not far away Devon was standing in the middle of a small gallery of men and women, swaying from side-to-side and for the first time in a long time singing acappella about the long walk home and the need to find your way.

Leland stared upward at the very spot that Aspasia had first appeared, and then he saw her again. Only this time there was only a trace of bone and wings, an outline free of colors and design. His body flexed and he yearned for a touch of feathers and the look of her piercing eyes. Offering neither, she hung there for seconds before disappearing again, most likely for good.

.

About the Author

Michael Croft is senior editor at *Narrative* and lives in his hometown of Reno, Nevada, where he worked in the casino industry for many years. He has publications with *Narrative*, *Prole* (UK), *The Pacific Review*, and several others.